STONE ARCH BOOKS
a capstone imprint

BATMAN
LI'L GOTHAM
™

▼▼ STONE ARCH BOOKS™

Published in 2015 by Stone Arch Books
A Capstone Imprint
1710 Roe Crest Drive
North Mankato, MN 56003
www.capstonepub.com

Originally published by DC Comics in the U.S. in single
magazine form as Batman: Li'l Gotham #9.
Copyright © 2015 DC Comics. All Rights Reserved.

DC Comics
1700 Broadway, New York, NY 10019
A Warner Bros. Entertainment Company
No part of this publication may be reproduced in
whole or in part, or stored in a retrieval system, or
transmitted in any form or by any means, electronic,
mechanical, photocopying, recording, or otherwise,
without written permission.

Cataloging-in-Publication Data is available at the
Library of Congress website:
ISBN: 978-1-4342-9736-5 (library binding)

Printed in China by Nordica.
0914/CA21401510
092014   008470NORDS15

Summary: When Batman and Robin chase the cunning
Clayface into Gotham City's biggest Comic-Con, they run
into security, other heroes, and trouble! And on Labor
Day, Jenna Duffy--carpenter to Gotham City's criminal
class--takes the day off. But will interruptions doom her
personal project?

STONE ARCH BOOKS
Ashley C. Andersen Zantop **Publisher**
Michael Dahl **Editorial Director**
Sean Tulien **Editor**
Heather Kindseth **Creative Director**
Bob Lentz **Art Director**
Hilary Wacholz and Peggie Carley **Designers**
Tori Abraham **Production Specialist**

DC Comics
Kristy Quinn **Original U.S. Editor**

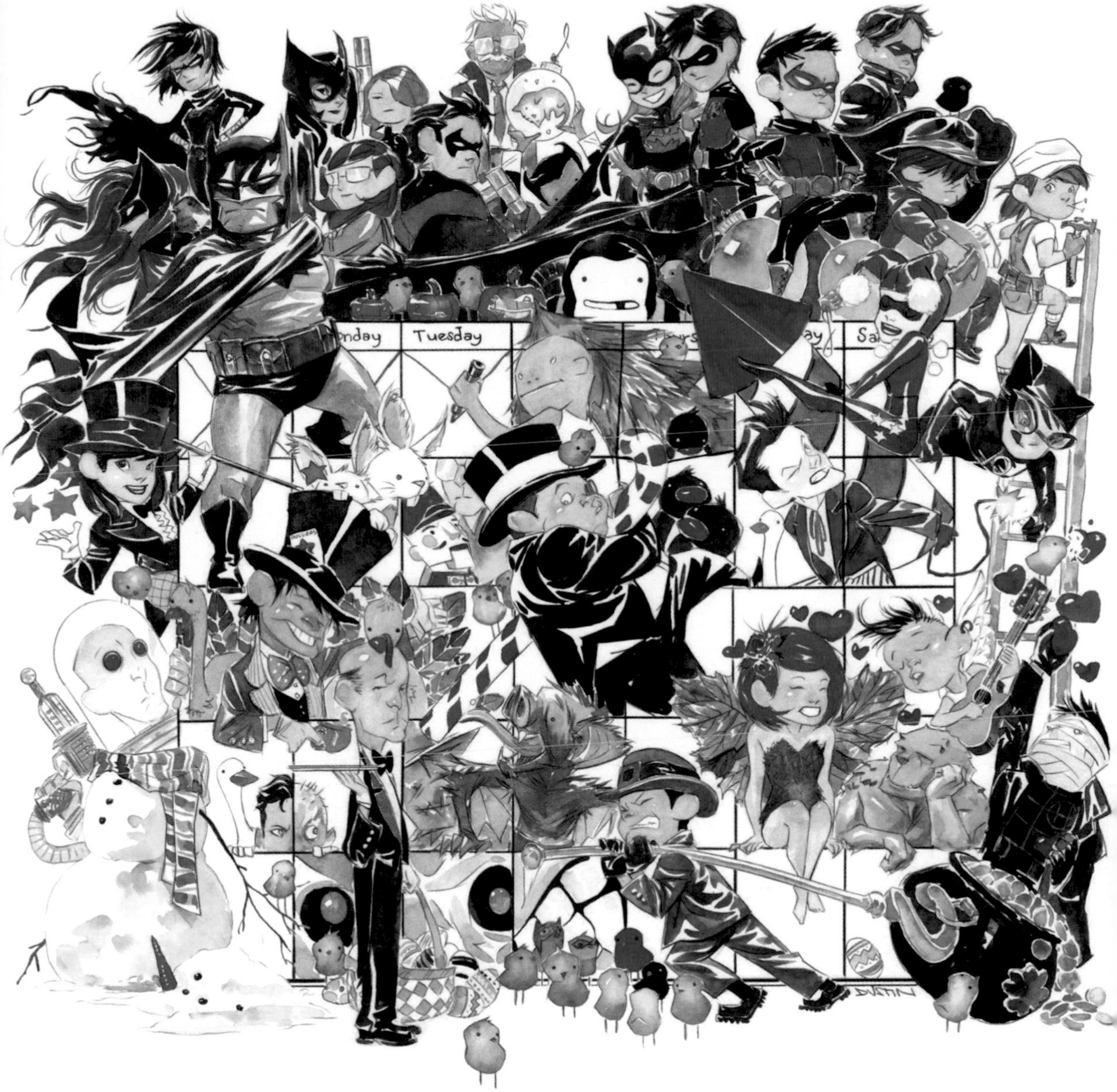
Tuesday
DUSTIN

COMIC CON AND LABOR DAY

Dustin Nguyen & Derek Fridolfs...................... writers
Dustin Nguyen.. artist
Saida Temofonte.. letterer

BATMAN created by
Bob Kane

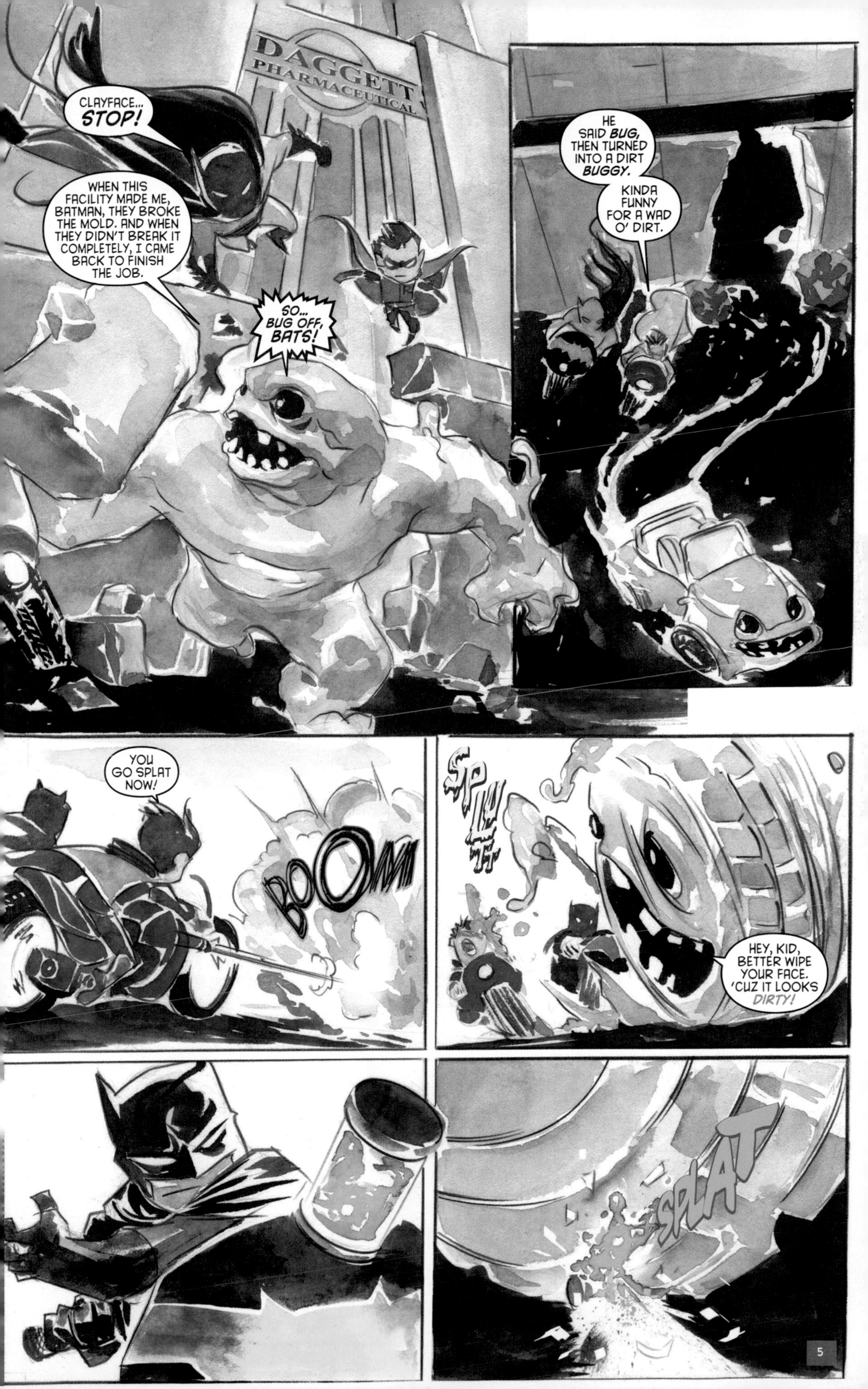
DAGGETT PHARMACEUTICAL
CLAYFACE... STOP!
WHEN THIS FACILITY MADE ME, BATMAN, THEY BROKE THE MOLD. AND WHEN THEY DIDN'T BREAK IT COMPLETELY, I CAME BACK TO FINISH THE JOB.
SO... BUG OFF, BATS!
HE SAID BUG, THEN TURNED INTO A DIRT BUGGY.
KINDA FUNNY FOR A WAD O' DIRT.
YOU GO SPLAT NOW!
BOOM
HEY, KID, BETTER WIPE YOUR FACE. 'CUZ IT LOOKS DIRTY!
SPLAT

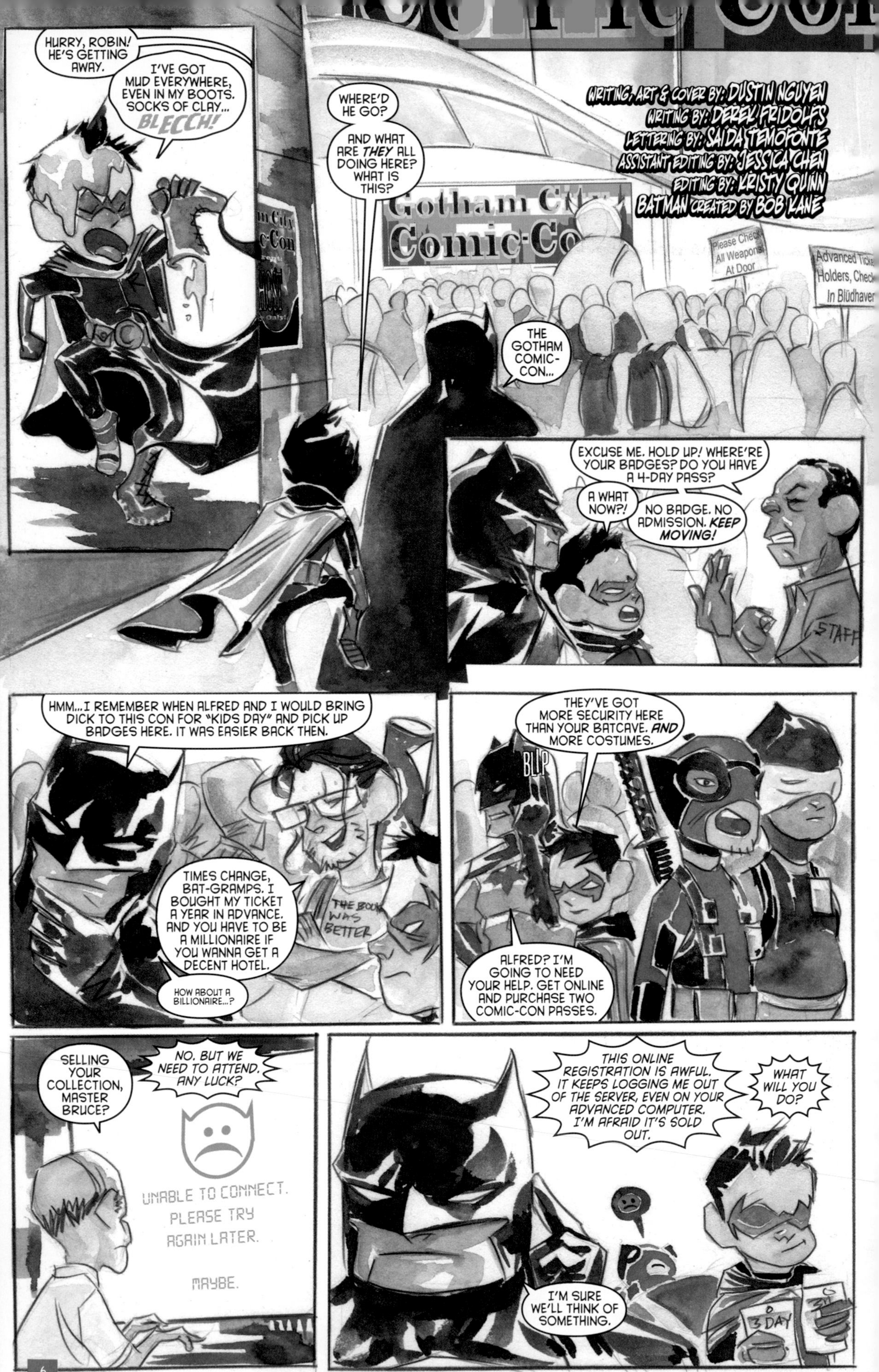
WRITING, ART & COVER BY: DUSTIN NGUYEN
WRITING BY: DEREK FRIDOLFS
LETTERING BY: SAIDA TEMOFONTE
ASSISTANT EDITING BY: JESSICA CHEN
EDITING BY: KRISTY QUINN
BATMAN CREATED BY BOB KANE
HURRY, ROBIN! HE'S GETTING AWAY.
I'VE GOT MUD EVERYWHERE, EVEN IN MY BOOTS. SOCKS OF CLAY... BLECCH!
WHERE'D HE GO?
AND WHAT ARE THEY ALL DOING HERE? WHAT IS THIS?
Gotham City Comic-Co
Please Check All Weapons At Door
Advanced Ticke Holders, Check In Blüdhaven
THE GOTHAM COMIC-CON...
EXCUSE ME. HOLD UP! WHERE'RE YOUR BADGES? DO YOU HAVE A 4-DAY PASS?
A WHAT NOW?!
NO BADGE. NO ADMISSION. KEEP MOVING!
STAFF
HMM...I REMEMBER WHEN ALFRED AND I WOULD BRING DICK TO THIS CON FOR "KIDS DAY" AND PICK UP BADGES HERE. IT WAS EASIER BACK THEN.
TIMES CHANGE, BAT-GRAMPS. I BOUGHT MY TICKET A YEAR IN ADVANCE. AND YOU HAVE TO BE A MILLIONAIRE IF YOU WANNA GET A DECENT HOTEL.
THE BOOK WAS BETTER
HOW ABOUT A BILLIONAIRE...?
THEY'VE GOT MORE SECURITY HERE THAN YOUR BATCAVE. AND MORE COSTUMES.
BLIP
ALFRED? I'M GOING TO NEED YOUR HELP. GET ONLINE AND PURCHASE TWO COMIC-CON PASSES.
SELLING YOUR COLLECTION, MASTER BRUCE?
NO. BUT WE NEED TO ATTEND. ANY LUCK?
UNABLE TO CONNECT. PLEASE TRY AGAIN LATER.
MAYBE.
THIS ONLINE REGISTRATION IS AWFUL. IT KEEPS LOGGING ME OUT OF THE SERVER, EVEN ON YOUR ADVANCED COMPUTER. I'M AFRAID IT'S SOLD OUT.
WHAT WILL YOU DO?
I'M SURE WE'LL THINK OF SOMETHING.
3 DAY

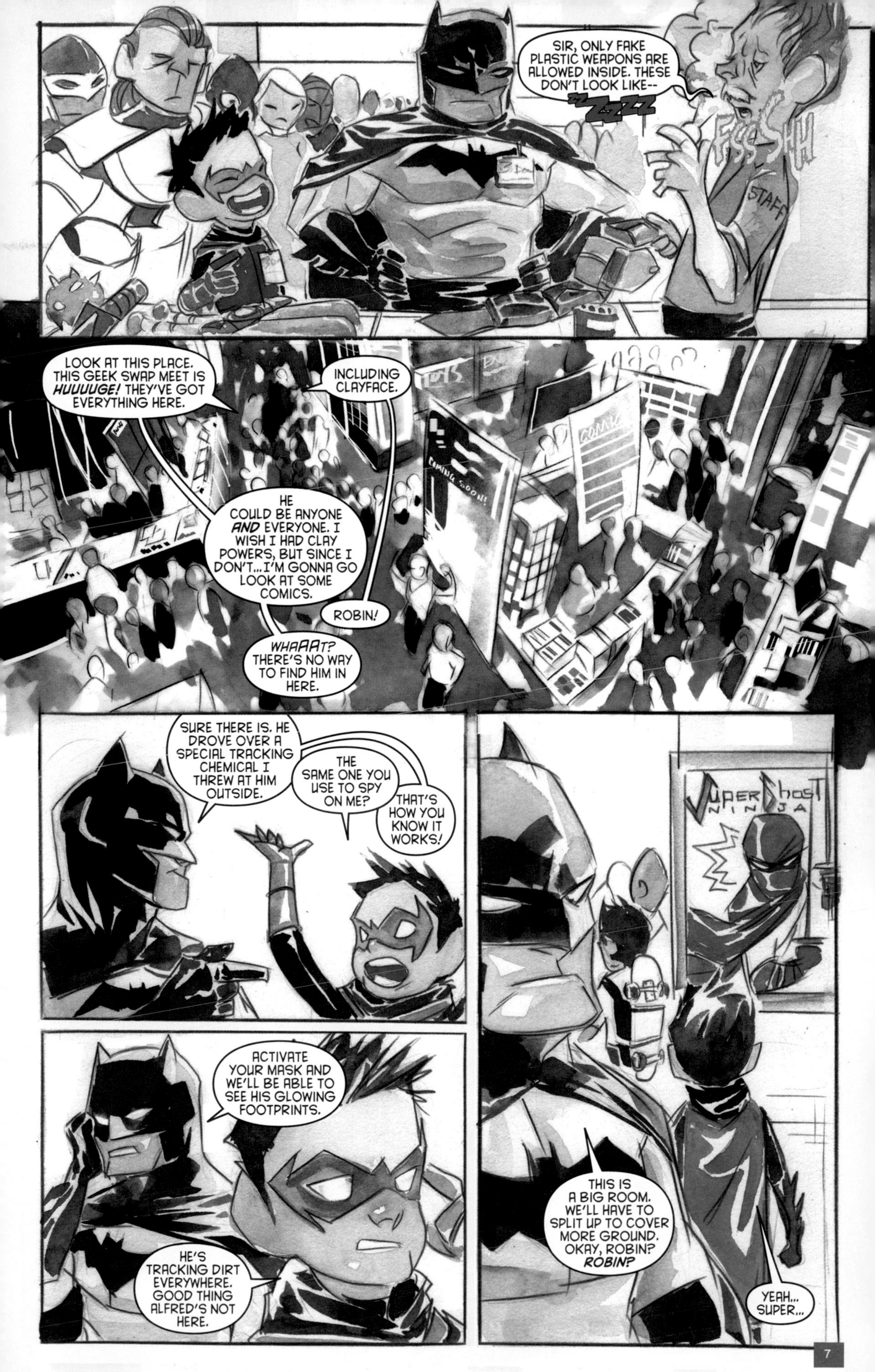
SIR, ONLY FAKE PLASTIC WEAPONS ARE ALLOWED INSIDE. THESE DON'T LOOK LIKE--
ZZZZ
FSSSHH
STAFF
LOOK AT THIS PLACE. THIS GEEK SWAP MEET IS HUUUUGE! THEY'VE GOT EVERYTHING HERE.
INCLUDING CLAYFACE.
HE COULD BE ANYONE AND EVERYONE. I WISH I HAD CLAY POWERS, BUT SINCE I DON'T...I'M GONNA GO LOOK AT SOME COMICS.
ROBIN!
WHAAAAT? THERE'S NO WAY TO FIND HIM IN HERE.
SURE THERE IS. HE DROVE OVER A SPECIAL TRACKING CHEMICAL I THREW AT HIM OUTSIDE.
THE SAME ONE YOU USE TO SPY ON ME?
THAT'S HOW YOU KNOW IT WORKS!
ACTIVATE YOUR MASK AND WE'LL BE ABLE TO SEE HIS GLOWING FOOTPRINTS.
HE'S TRACKING DIRT EVERYWHERE. GOOD THING ALFRED'S NOT HERE.
SUPER GHOST NINJA
THIS IS A BIG ROOM. WE'LL HAVE TO SPLIT UP TO COVER MORE GROUND. OKAY, ROBIN? ROBIN?
YEAH... SUPER...

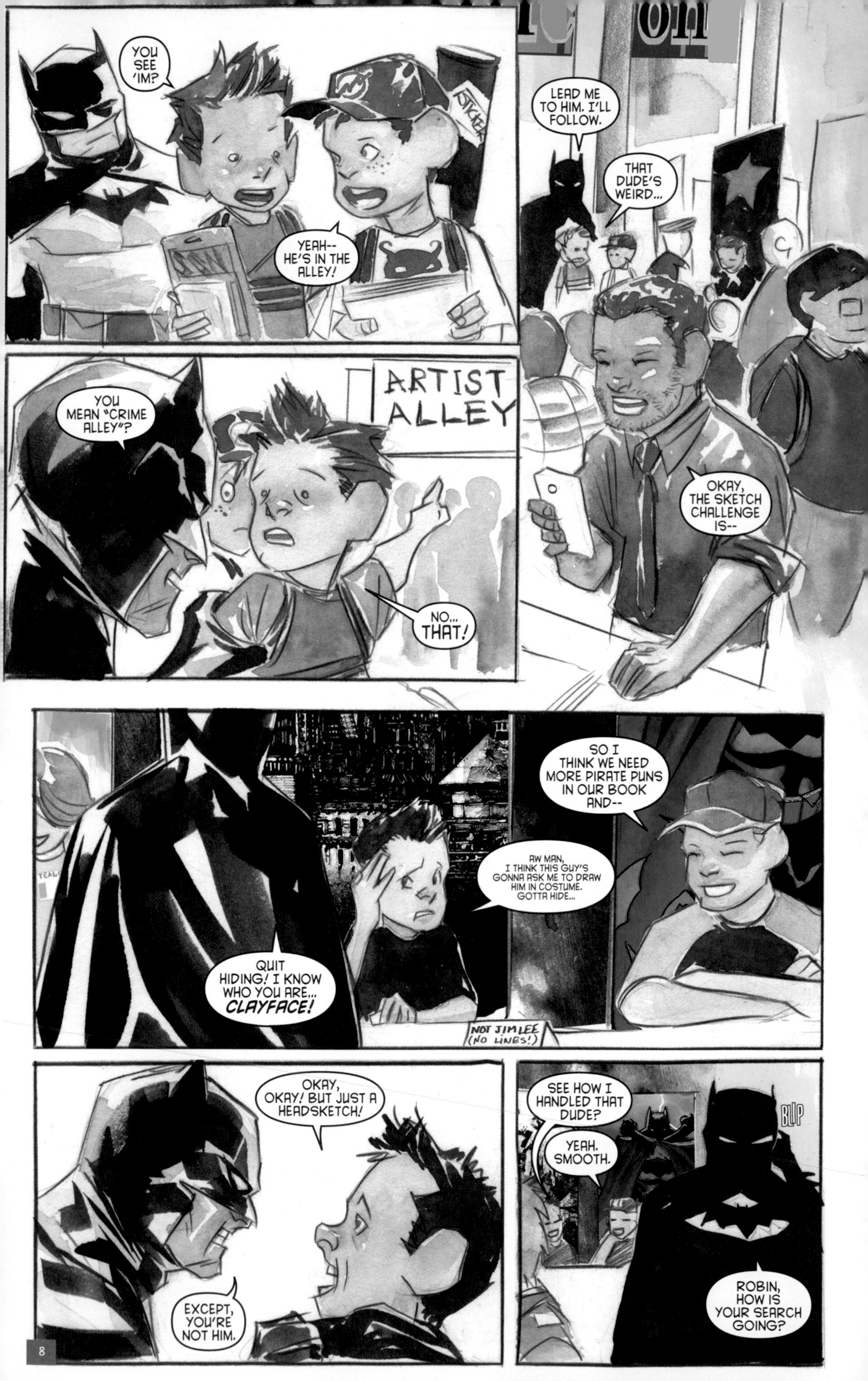
YOU SEE 'IM?
YEAH-- HE'S IN THE ALLEY!
LEAD ME TO HIM. I'LL FOLLOW.
THAT DUDE'S WEIRD...
YOU MEAN "CRIME ALLEY"?
ARTIST ALLEY
NO... THAT!
OKAY, THE SKETCH CHALLENGE IS--
QUIT HIDING! I KNOW WHO YOU ARE... CLAYFACE!
AW MAN, I THINK THIS GUY'S GONNA ASK ME TO DRAW HIM IN COSTUME. GOTTA HIDE...
SO I THINK WE NEED MORE PIRATE PUNS IN OUR BOOK AND--
NOT JIM LEE (NO LINES!)
OKAY, OKAY! BUT JUST A HEADSKETCH!
EXCEPT, YOU'RE NOT HIM.
SEE HOW I HANDLED THAT DUDE?
YEAH. SMOOTH.
BLIP
ROBIN, HOW IS YOUR SEARCH GOING?

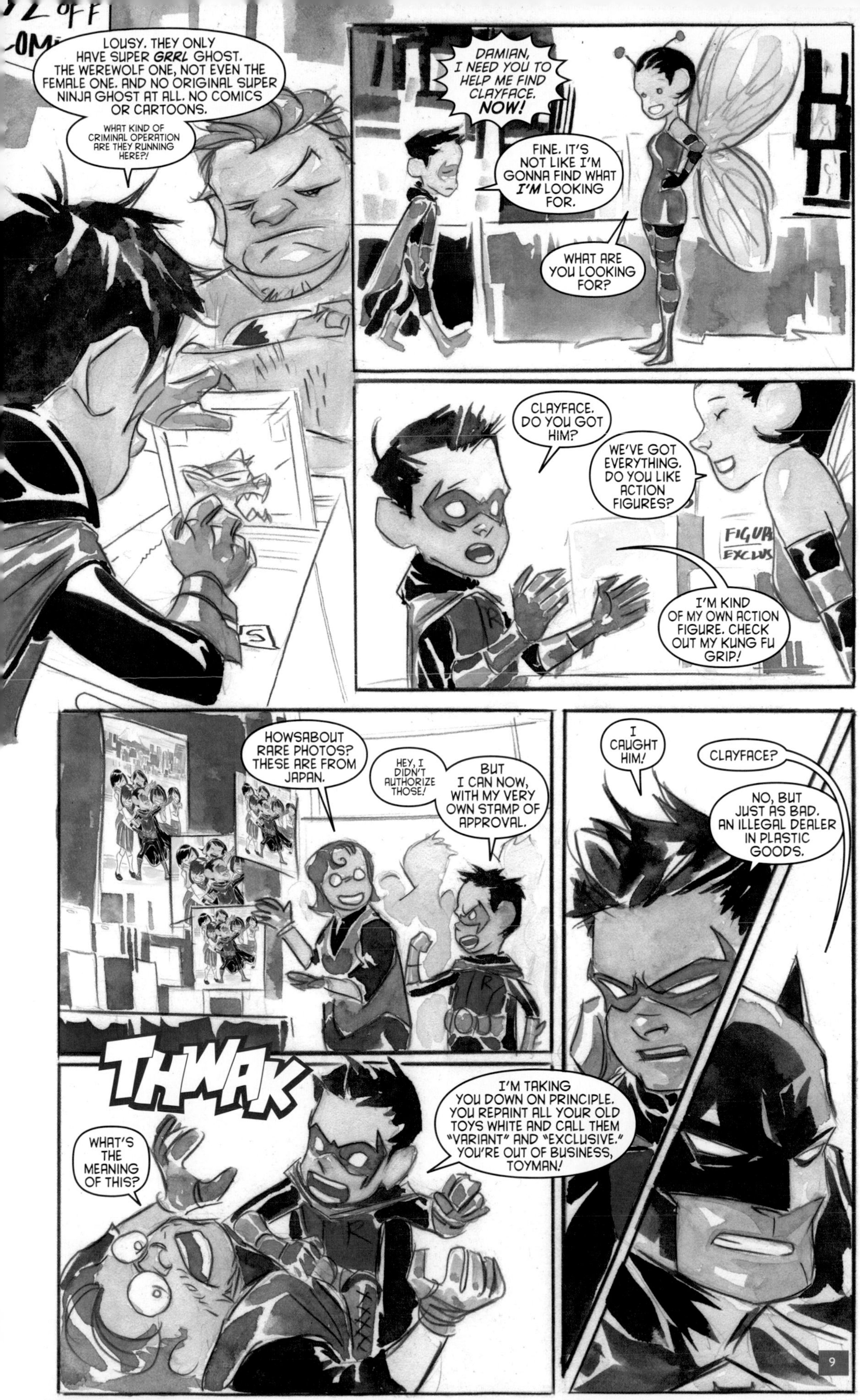
LOUSY. THEY ONLY HAVE SUPER GRRL GHOST. THE WEREWOLF ONE, NOT EVEN THE FEMALE ONE. AND NO ORIGINAL SUPER NINJA GHOST AT ALL. NO COMICS OR CARTOONS.
WHAT KIND OF CRIMINAL OPERATION ARE THEY RUNNING HERE?!
DAMIAN, I NEED YOU TO HELP ME FIND CLAYFACE. NOW!
FINE. IT'S NOT LIKE I'M GONNA FIND WHAT I'M LOOKING FOR.
WHAT ARE YOU LOOKING FOR?
CLAYFACE. DO YOU GOT HIM?
WE'VE GOT EVERYTHING. DO YOU LIKE ACTION FIGURES?
I'M KIND OF MY OWN ACTION FIGURE. CHECK OUT MY KUNG FU GRIP!
HOWSABOUT RARE PHOTOS? THESE ARE FROM JAPAN.
HEY, I DIDN'T AUTHORIZE THOSE!
BUT I CAN NOW, WITH MY VERY OWN STAMP OF APPROVAL.
THWAK
WHAT'S THE MEANING OF THIS?
I'M TAKING YOU DOWN ON PRINCIPLE. YOU REPAINT ALL YOUR OLD TOYS WHITE AND CALL THEM "VARIANT" AND "EXCLUSIVE." YOU'RE OUT OF BUSINESS, TOYMAN!
I CAUGHT HIM!
CLAYFACE?
NO, BUT JUST AS BAD. AN ILLEGAL DEALER IN PLASTIC GOODS.

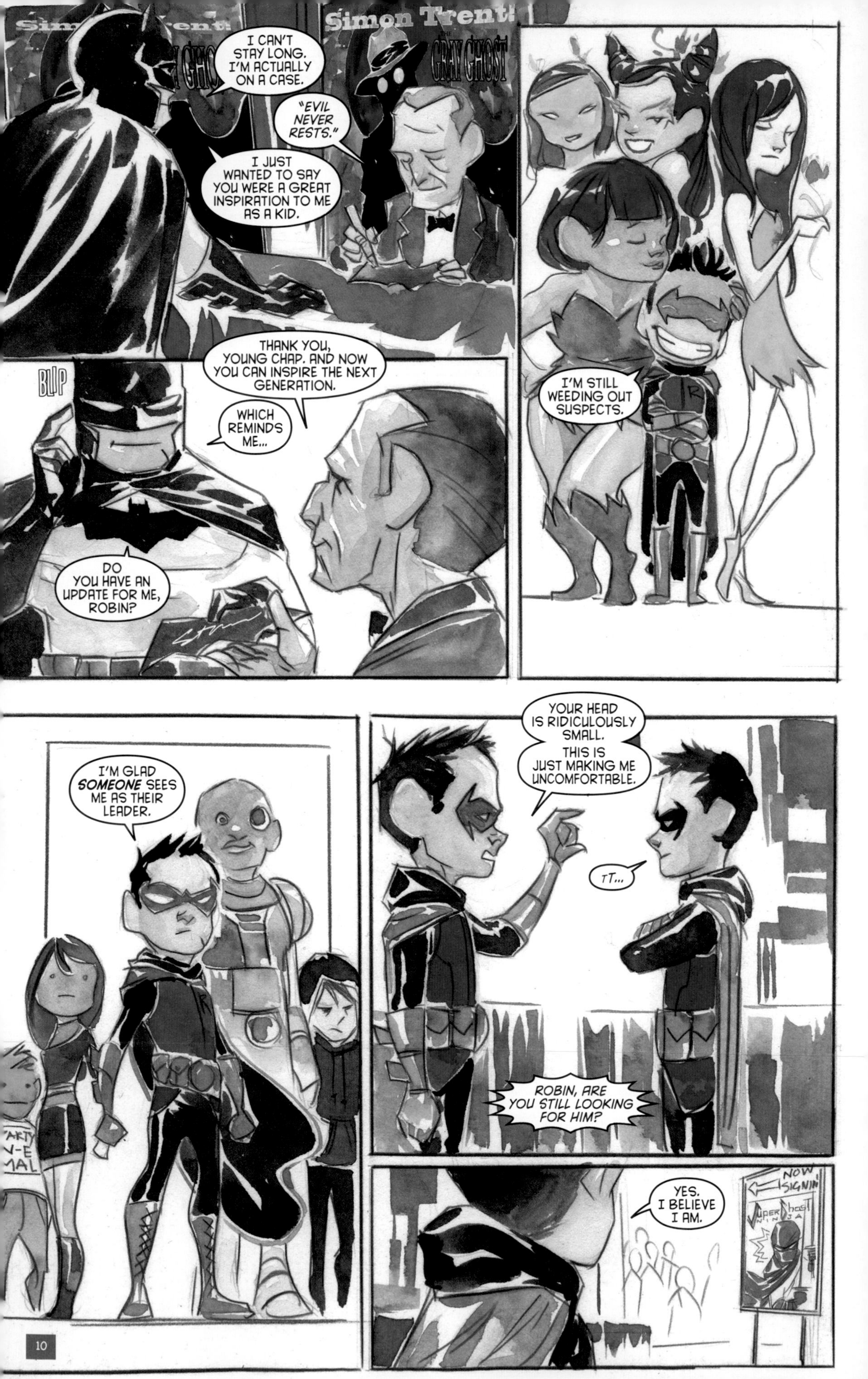
Simon Trent: The Gray Ghost
I CAN'T STAY LONG. I'M ACTUALLY ON A CASE.
"EVIL NEVER RESTS."
I JUST WANTED TO SAY YOU WERE A GREAT INSPIRATION TO ME AS A KID.
I'M STILL WEEDING OUT SUSPECTS.
THANK YOU, YOUNG CHAP. AND NOW YOU CAN INSPIRE THE NEXT GENERATION.
BLIP
WHICH REMINDS ME...
DO YOU HAVE AN UPDATE FOR ME, ROBIN?
I'M GLAD *SOMEONE* SEES ME AS THEIR LEADER.
YOUR HEAD IS RIDICULOUSLY SMALL.
THIS IS JUST MAKING ME UNCOMFORTABLE.
TT...
ROBIN, ARE YOU STILL LOOKING FOR HIM?
YES. I BELIEVE I AM.
NOW SIGNIN'
Super Ghost Ninja

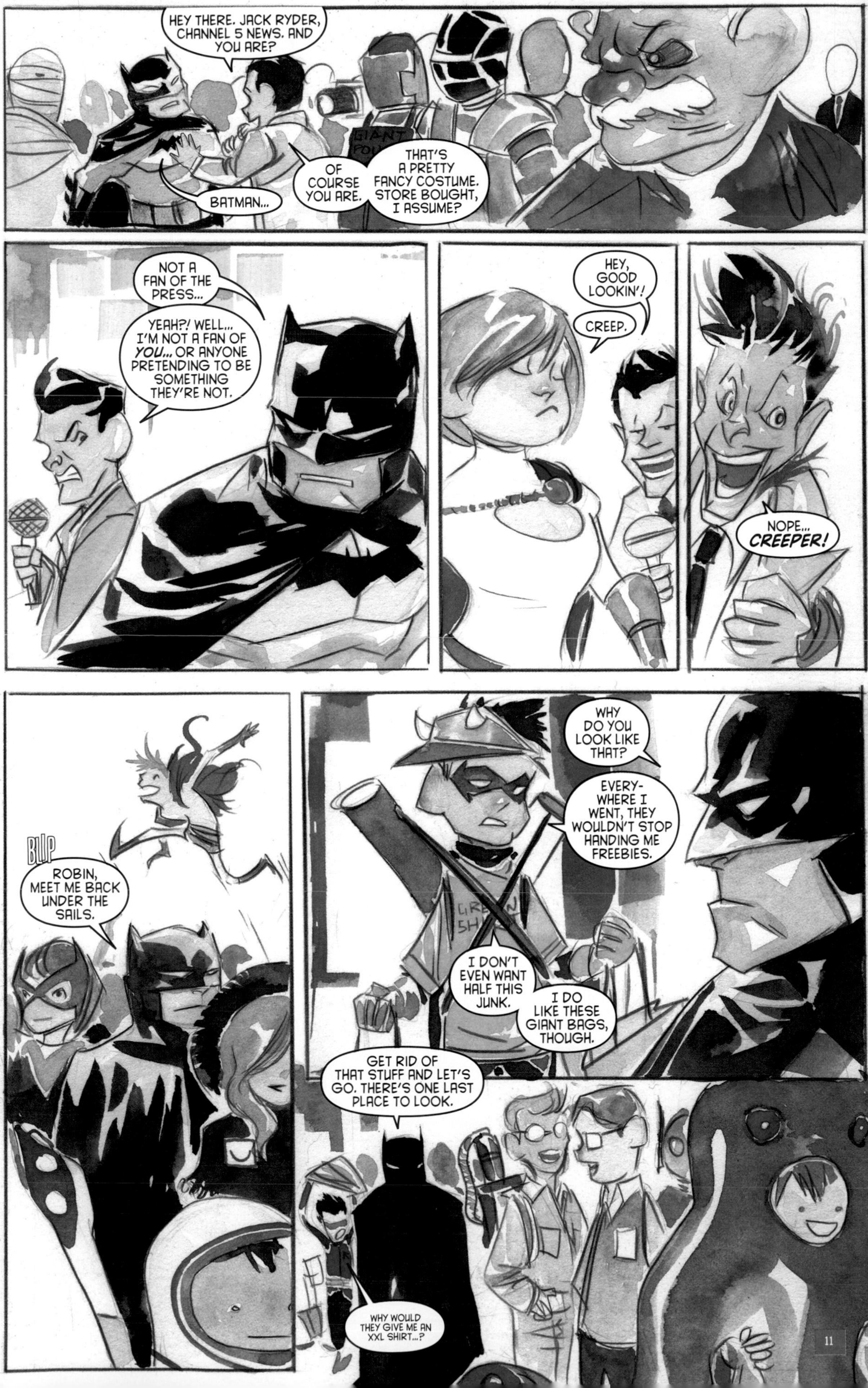
HEY THERE. JACK RYDER, CHANNEL 5 NEWS. AND YOU ARE?
BATMAN...
OF COURSE YOU ARE.
THAT'S A PRETTY FANCY COSTUME. STORE BOUGHT, I ASSUME?
NOT A FAN OF THE PRESS...
YEAH?! WELL... I'M NOT A FAN OF *YOU*... OR ANYONE PRETENDING TO BE SOMETHING THEY'RE NOT.
HEY, GOOD LOOKIN'!
CREEP.
NOPE... **CREEPER!**
BLIP
ROBIN, MEET ME BACK UNDER THE SAILS.
WHY DO YOU LOOK LIKE THAT?
EVERY-WHERE I WENT, THEY WOULDN'T STOP HANDING ME FREEBIES.
I DON'T EVEN WANT HALF THIS JUNK.
I DO LIKE THESE GIANT BAGS, THOUGH.
GET RID OF THAT STUFF AND LET'S GO. THERE'S ONE LAST PLACE TO LOOK.
WHY WOULD THEY GIVE ME AN XXL SHIRT...?

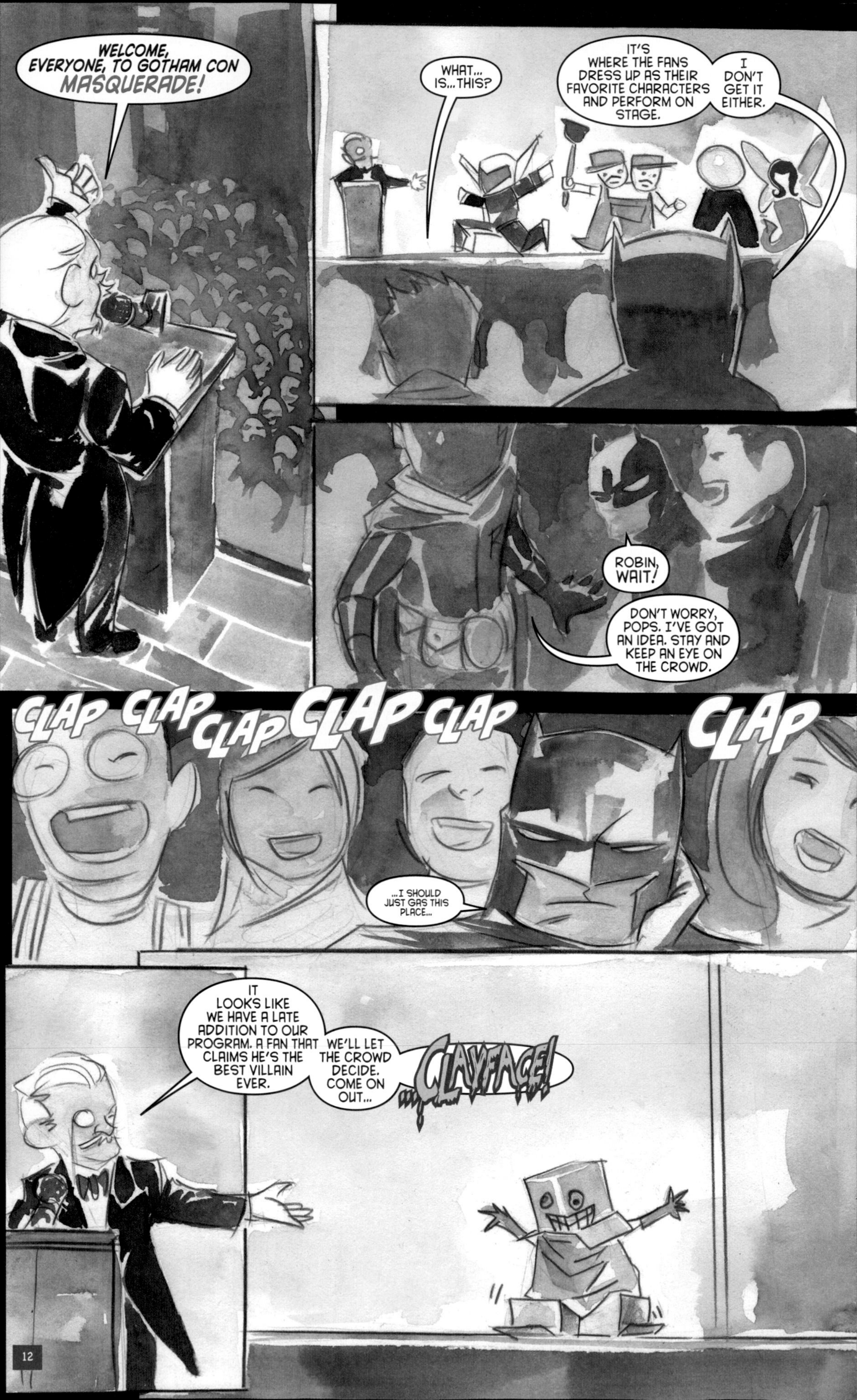

WELCOME, EVERYONE, TO GOTHAM CON MASQUERADE!
WHAT... IS...THIS?
IT'S WHERE THE FANS DRESS UP AS THEIR FAVORITE CHARACTERS AND PERFORM ON STAGE.
I DON'T GET IT EITHER.
ROBIN, WAIT!
DON'T WORRY, POPS. I'VE GOT AN IDEA. STAY AND KEEP AN EYE ON THE CROWD.
CLAP CLAP CLAP CLAP CLAP CLAP
...I SHOULD JUST GAS THIS PLACE...
IT LOOKS LIKE WE HAVE A LATE ADDITION TO OUR PROGRAM. A FAN THAT CLAIMS HE'S THE BEST VILLAIN EVER.
WE'LL LET THE CROWD DECIDE. COME ON OUT...
...CLAYFACE!

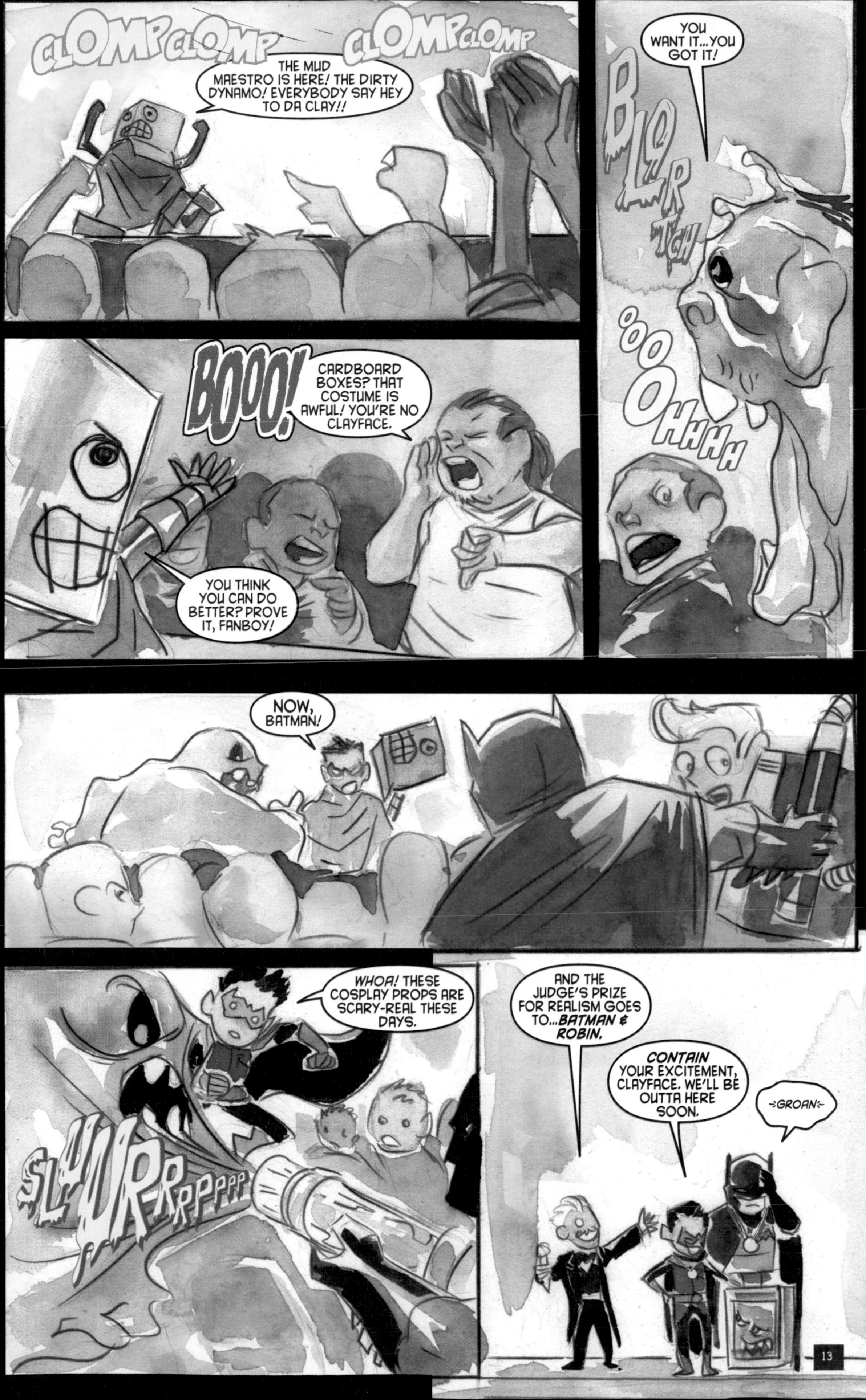

CLOMP CLOMP CLOMP CLOMP
THE MUD MAESTRO IS HERE! THE DIRTY DYNAMO! EVERYBODY SAY HEY TO DA CLAY!!
YOU WANT IT...YOU GOT IT!
BLORTCH
OOOOHHHHH
BOOO!
CARDBOARD BOXES? THAT COSTUME IS AWFUL! YOU'RE NO CLAYFACE.
YOU THINK YOU CAN DO BETTER? PROVE IT, FANBOY!
NOW, BATMAN!
WHOA! THESE COSPLAY PROPS ARE SCARY-REAL THESE DAYS.
SLURRRPPPP
AND THE JUDGE'S PRIZE FOR REALISM GOES TO...BATMAN & ROBIN.
CONTAIN YOUR EXCITEMENT, CLAYFACE. WE'LL BE OUTTA HERE SOON.
GROAN

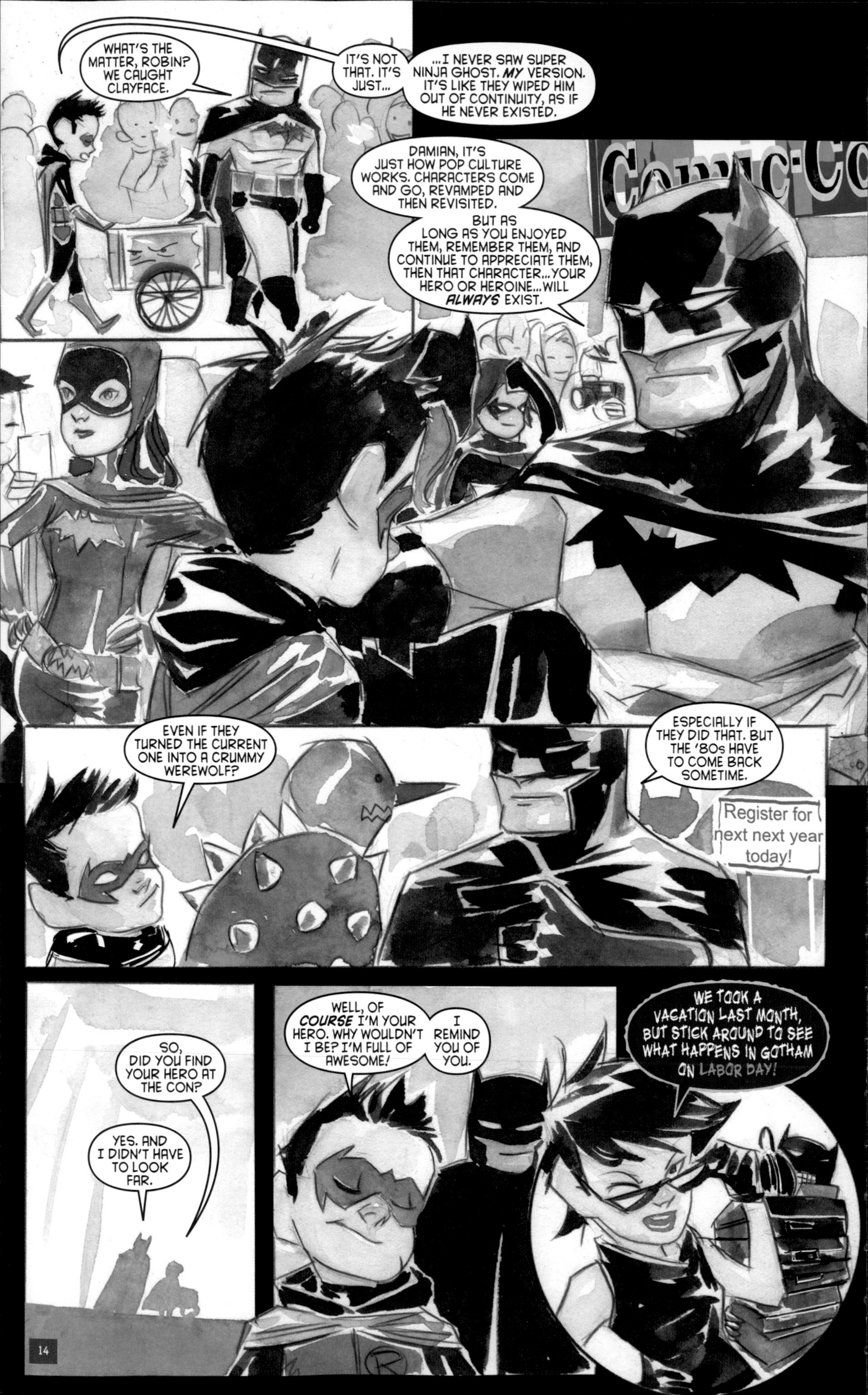
WHAT'S THE MATTER, ROBIN? WE CAUGHT CLAYFACE.
IT'S NOT THAT. IT'S JUST...
...I NEVER SAW SUPER NINJA GHOST. MY VERSION. IT'S LIKE THEY WIPED HIM OUT OF CONTINUITY, AS IF HE NEVER EXISTED.
Comic-Co
DAMIAN, IT'S JUST HOW POP CULTURE WORKS. CHARACTERS COME AND GO, REVAMPED AND THEN REVISITED.
BUT AS LONG AS YOU ENJOYED THEM, REMEMBER THEM, AND CONTINUE TO APPRECIATE THEM, THEN THAT CHARACTER...YOUR HERO OR HEROINE...WILL ALWAYS EXIST.
EVEN IF THEY TURNED THE CURRENT ONE INTO A CRUMMY WEREWOLF?
ESPECIALLY IF THEY DID THAT. BUT THE '80s HAVE TO COME BACK SOMETIME.
Register for next next year today!
SO, DID YOU FIND YOUR HERO AT THE CON?
YES. AND I DIDN'T HAVE TO LOOK FAR.
WELL, OF COURSE I'M YOUR HERO. WHY WOULDN'T I BE? I'M FULL OF AWESOME!
I REMIND YOU OF YOU.
WE TOOK A VACATION LAST MONTH, BUT STICK AROUND TO SEE WHAT HAPPENS IN GOTHAM ON LABOR DAY!

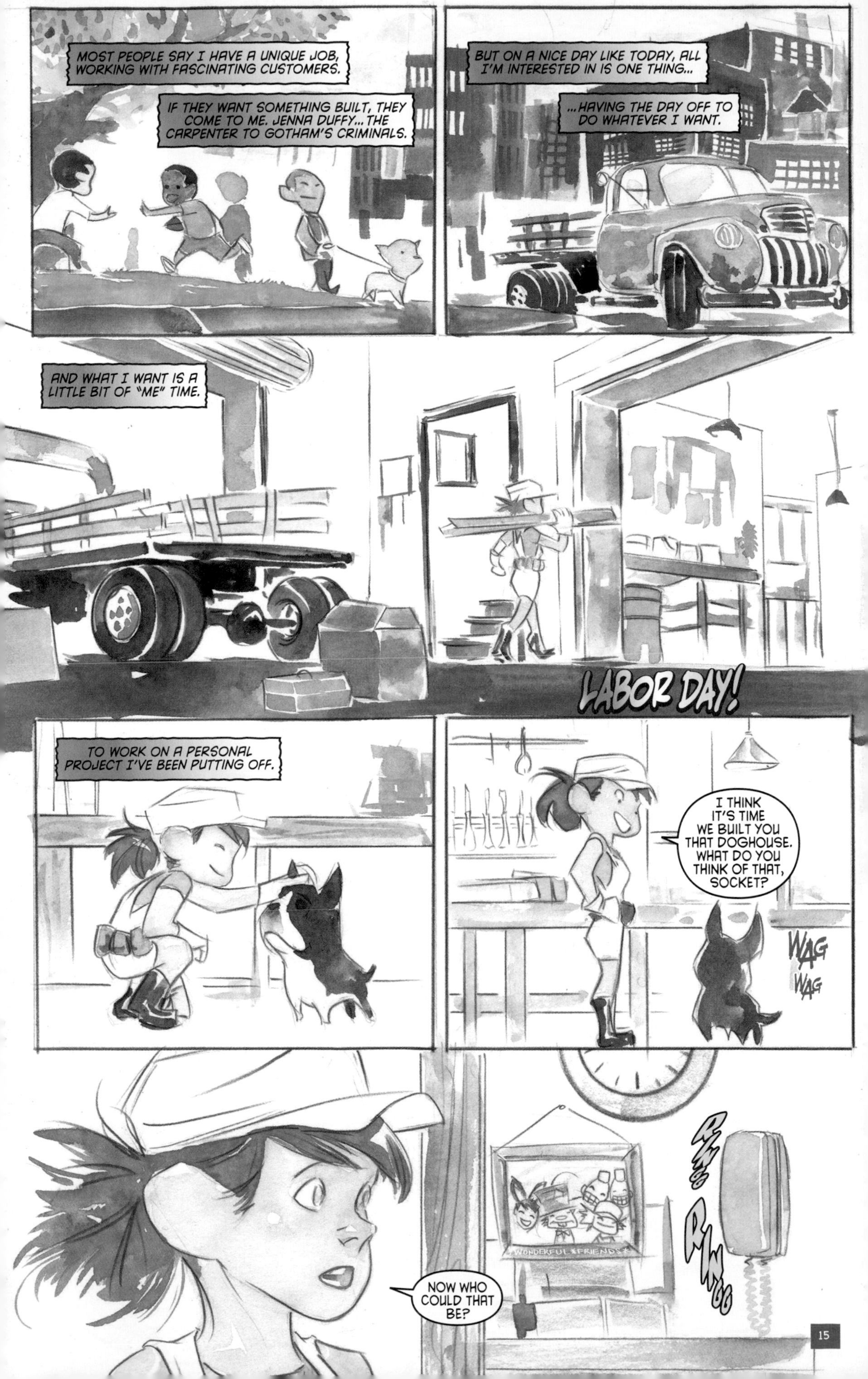
MOST PEOPLE SAY I HAVE A UNIQUE JOB, WORKING WITH FASCINATING CUSTOMERS.
IF THEY WANT SOMETHING BUILT, THEY COME TO ME. JENNA DUFFY... THE CARPENTER TO GOTHAM'S CRIMINALS.
BUT ON A NICE DAY LIKE TODAY, ALL I'M INTERESTED IN IS ONE THING...
...HAVING THE DAY OFF TO DO WHATEVER I WANT.
AND WHAT I WANT IS A LITTLE BIT OF "ME" TIME.
LABOR DAY!
TO WORK ON A PERSONAL PROJECT I'VE BEEN PUTTING OFF.
I THINK IT'S TIME WE BUILT YOU THAT DOGHOUSE. WHAT DO YOU THINK OF THAT, SOCKET?
WAG
WAG
WONDERFUL FRIENDS
RINGG
RINGG
NOW WHO COULD THAT BE?

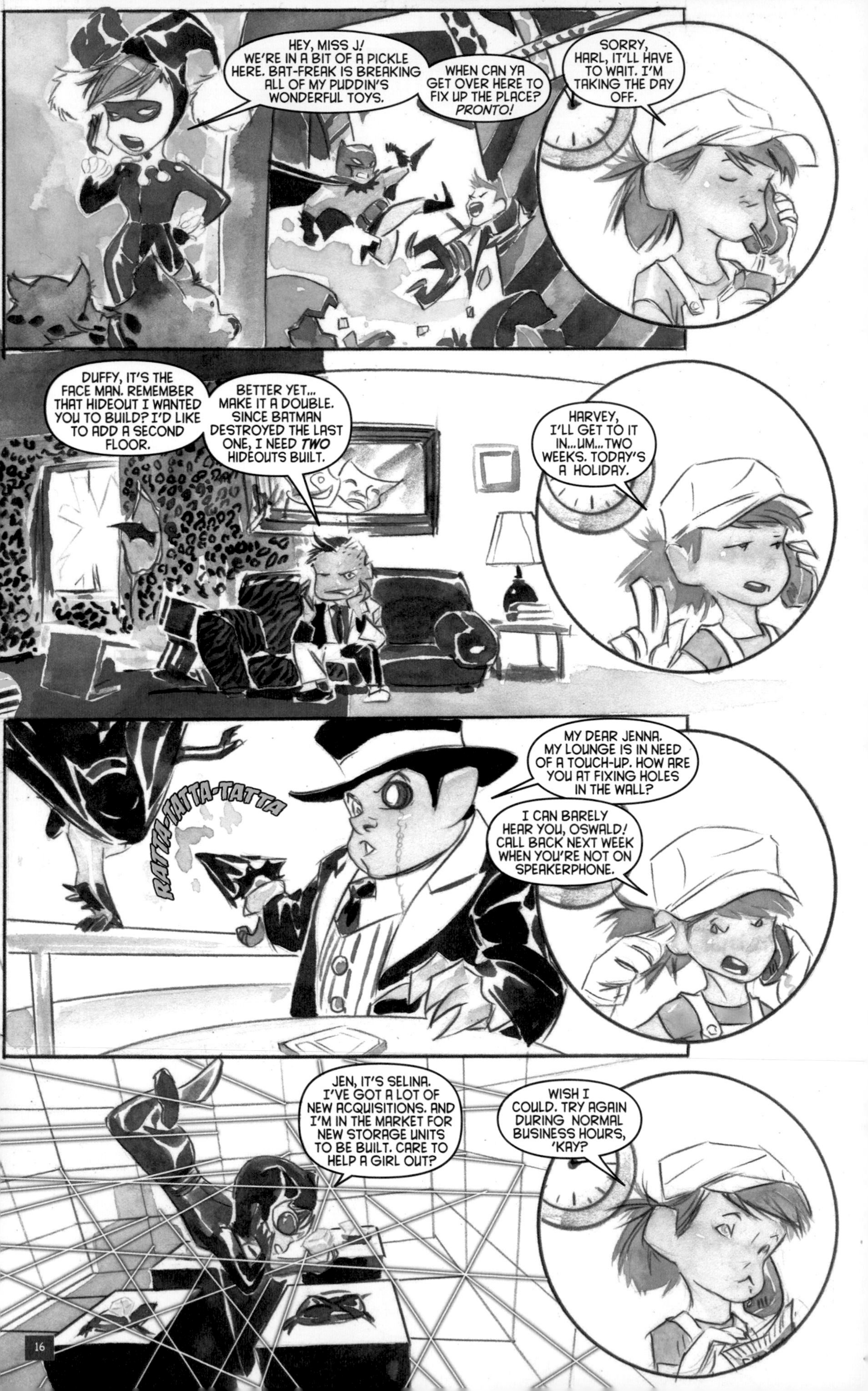
HEY, MISS J! WE'RE IN A BIT OF A PICKLE HERE. BAT-FREAK IS BREAKING ALL OF MY PUDDIN'S WONDERFUL TOYS.
WHEN CAN YA GET OVER HERE TO FIX UP THE PLACE? *PRONTO!*
SORRY, HARL, IT'LL HAVE TO WAIT. I'M TAKING THE DAY OFF.
DUFFY, IT'S THE FACE MAN. REMEMBER THAT HIDEOUT I WANTED YOU TO BUILD? I'D LIKE TO ADD A SECOND FLOOR.
BETTER YET... MAKE IT A DOUBLE. SINCE BATMAN DESTROYED THE LAST ONE, I NEED *TWO* HIDEOUTS BUILT.
HARVEY, I'LL GET TO IT IN...UM...TWO WEEKS. TODAY'S A HOLIDAY.
RATTA-TATTA-TATTA
MY DEAR JENNA. MY LOUNGE IS IN NEED OF A TOUCH-UP. HOW ARE YOU AT FIXING HOLES IN THE WALL?
I CAN BARELY HEAR YOU, OSWALD! CALL BACK NEXT WEEK WHEN YOU'RE NOT ON SPEAKERPHONE.
JEN, IT'S SELINA. I'VE GOT A LOT OF NEW ACQUISITIONS. AND I'M IN THE MARKET FOR NEW STORAGE UNITS TO BE BUILT. CARE TO HELP A GIRL OUT?
WISH I COULD. TRY AGAIN DURING NORMAL BUSINESS HOURS, 'KAY?

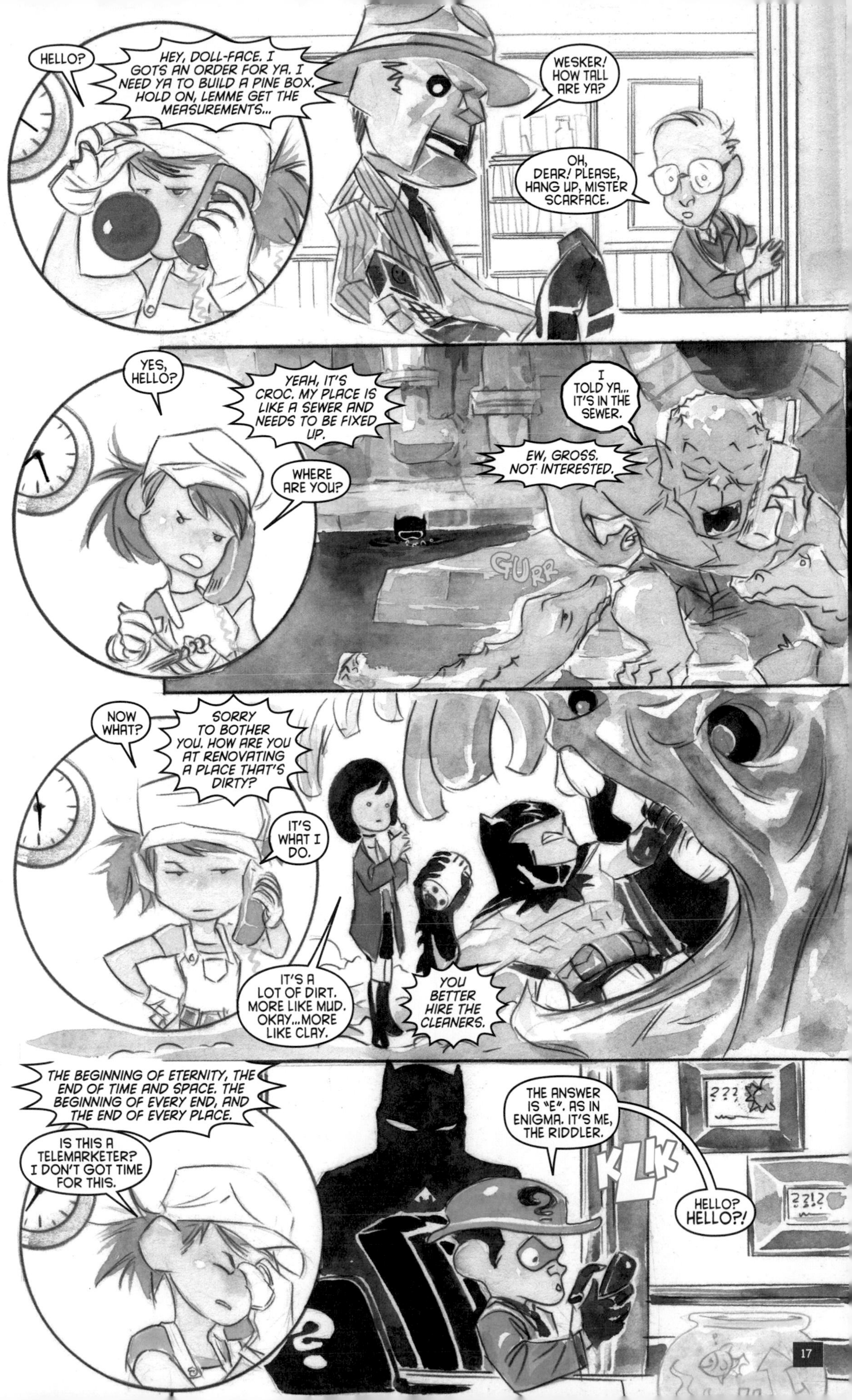
HELLO?
HEY, DOLL-FACE. I GOTS AN ORDER FOR YA. I NEED YA TO BUILD A PINE BOX. HOLD ON, LEMME GET THE MEASUREMENTS...
WESKER! HOW TALL ARE YA?
OH, DEAR! PLEASE, HANG UP, MISTER SCARFACE.
YES, HELLO?
YEAH, IT'S CROC. MY PLACE IS LIKE A SEWER AND NEEDS TO BE FIXED UP.
WHERE ARE YOU?
I TOLD YA... IT'S IN THE SEWER.
EW, GROSS. NOT INTERESTED.
GURR
NOW WHAT?
SORRY TO BOTHER YOU. HOW ARE YOU AT RENOVATING A PLACE THAT'S DIRTY?
IT'S WHAT I DO.
IT'S A LOT OF DIRT. MORE LIKE MUD. OKAY...MORE LIKE CLAY.
YOU BETTER HIRE THE CLEANERS.
THE BEGINNING OF ETERNITY, THE END OF TIME AND SPACE. THE BEGINNING OF EVERY END, AND THE END OF EVERY PLACE.
IS THIS A TELEMARKETER? I DON'T GOT TIME FOR THIS.
THE ANSWER IS "E". AS IN ENIGMA. IT'S ME, THE RIDDLER.
KLIK
HELLO? HELLO?!

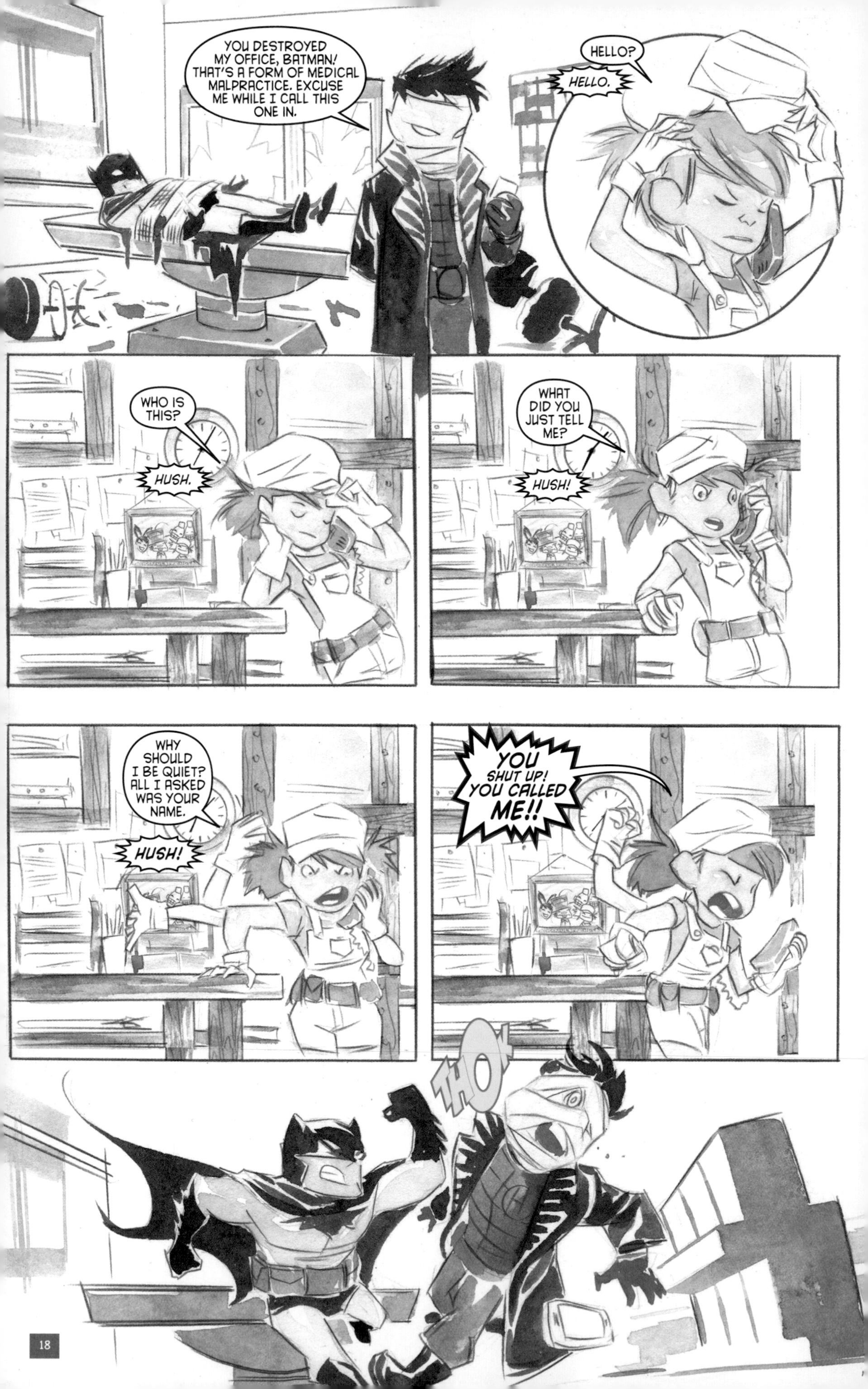
YOU DESTROYED MY OFFICE, BATMAN! THAT'S A FORM OF MEDICAL MALPRACTICE. EXCUSE ME WHILE I CALL THIS ONE IN.
HELLO?
HELLO.
WHO IS THIS?
HUSH.
WHAT DID YOU JUST TELL ME?
HUSH!
WHY SHOULD I BE QUIET? ALL I ASKED WAS YOUR NAME.
HUSH!
YOU SHUT UP! YOU CALLED ME!!
THOK

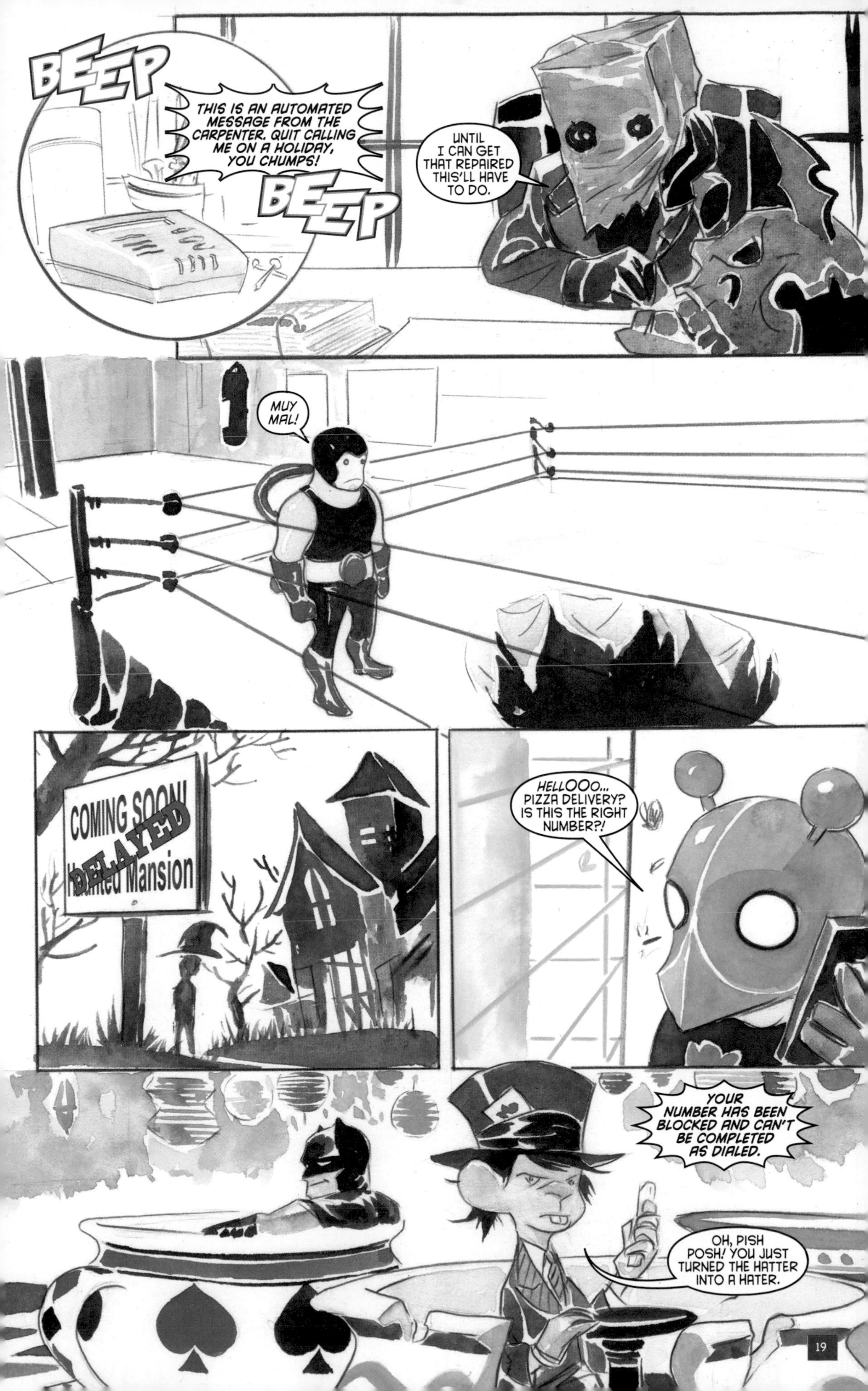
BEEP
THIS IS AN AUTOMATED MESSAGE FROM THE CARPENTER. QUIT CALLING ME ON A HOLIDAY, YOU CHUMPS!
BEEP
UNTIL I CAN GET THAT REPAIRED THIS'LL HAVE TO DO.
MUY MAL!
COMING SOON!
DELAYED
Haunted Mansion
HELLOOo... PIZZA DELIVERY? IS THIS THE RIGHT NUMBER?!
YOUR NUMBER HAS BEEN BLOCKED AND CAN'T BE COMPLETED AS DIALED.
OH, PISH POSH! YOU JUST TURNED THE HATTER INTO A HATER.

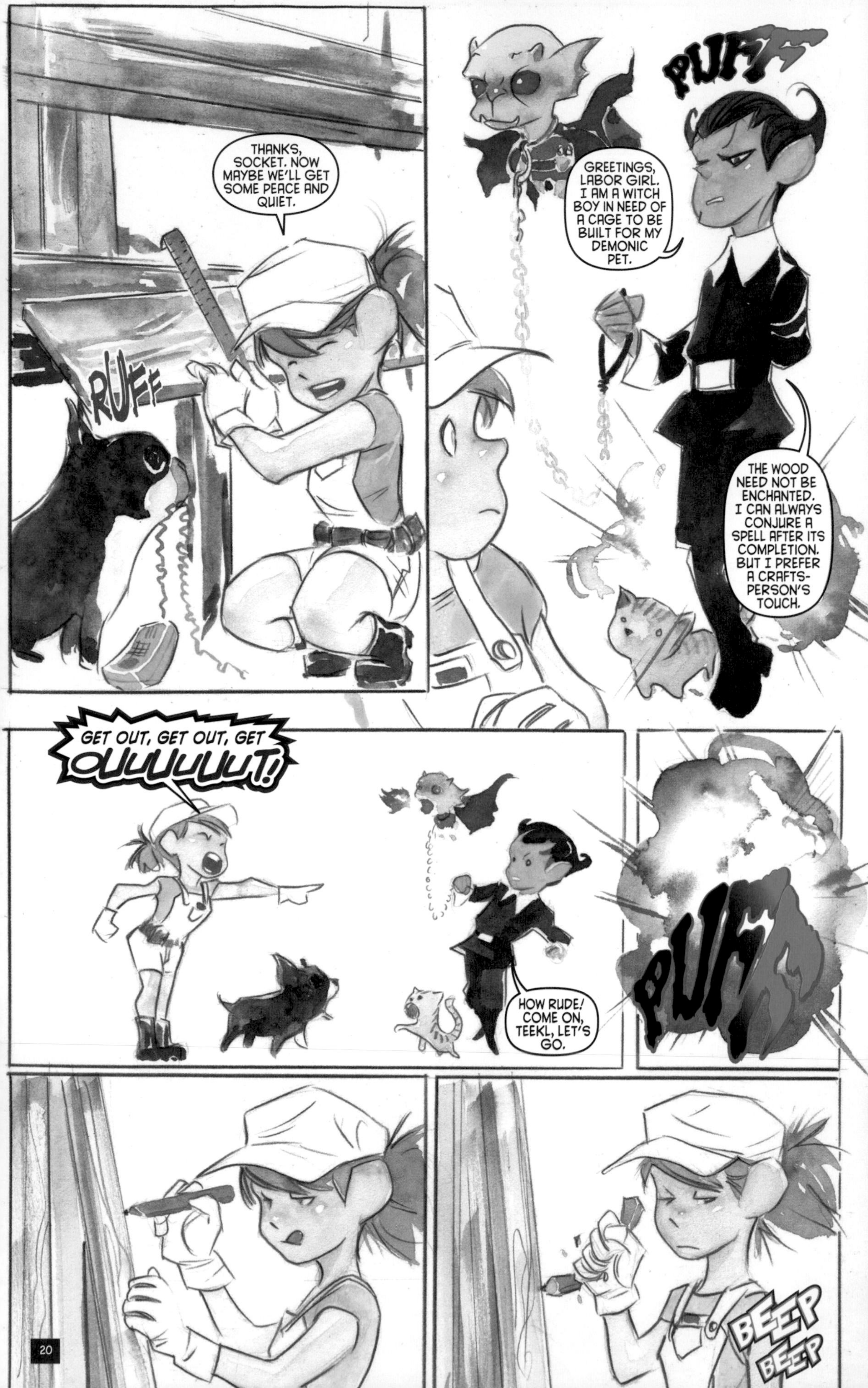
THANKS, SOCKET. NOW MAYBE WE'LL GET SOME PEACE AND QUIET.
RUFF
PUFF
GREETINGS, LABOR GIRL. I AM A WITCH BOY IN NEED OF A CAGE TO BE BUILT FOR MY DEMONIC PET.
THE WOOD NEED NOT BE ENCHANTED. I CAN ALWAYS CONJURE A SPELL AFTER ITS COMPLETION. BUT I PREFER A CRAFTS-PERSON'S TOUCH.
GET OUT, GET OUT, GET OUUUUUUT!
HOW RUDE! COME ON, TEEKL, LET'S GO.
PUFF
BEEP BEEP

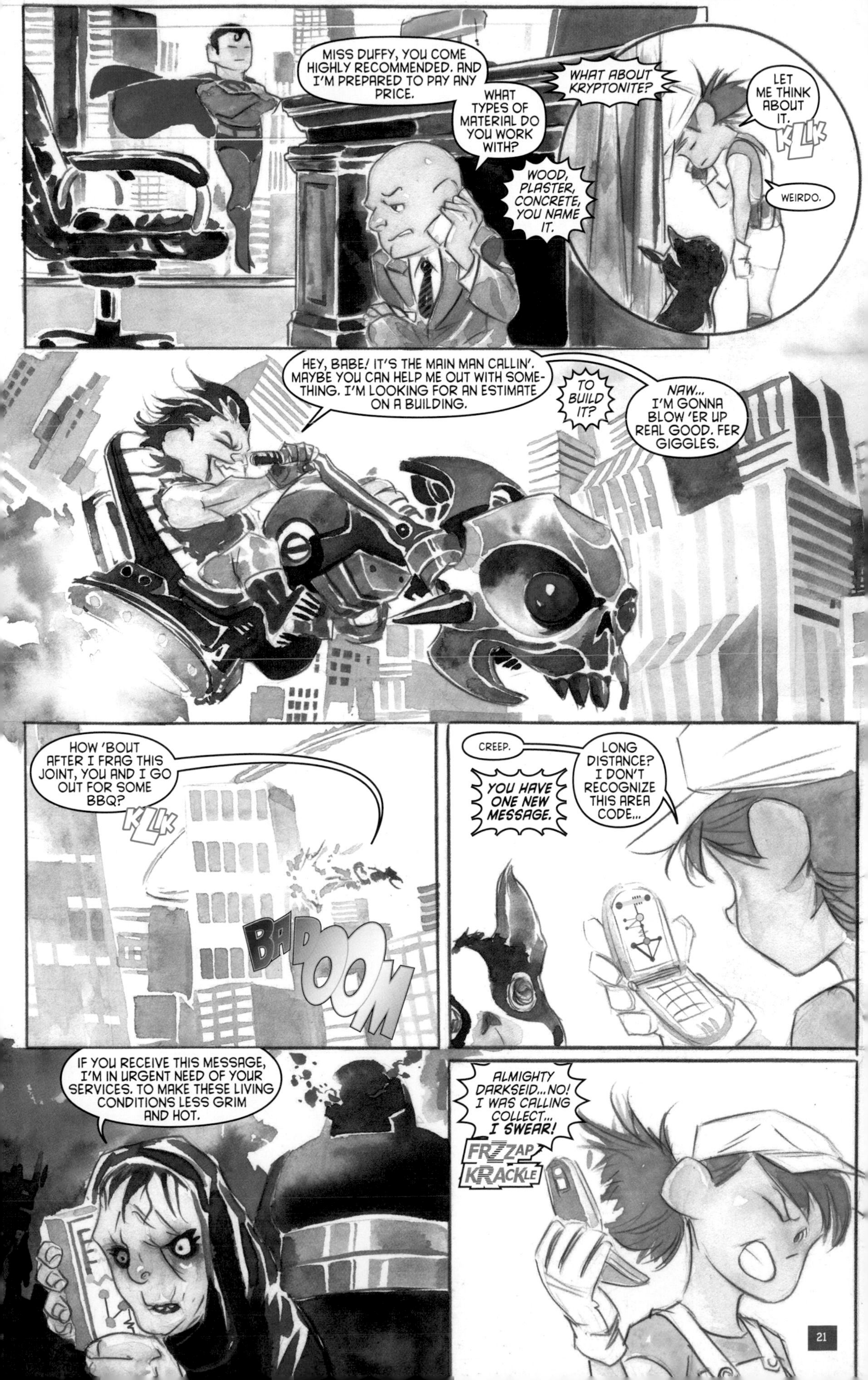
MISS DUFFY, YOU COME HIGHLY RECOMMENDED. AND I'M PREPARED TO PAY ANY PRICE.
WHAT TYPES OF MATERIAL DO YOU WORK WITH?
WOOD, PLASTER, CONCRETE, YOU NAME IT.
WHAT ABOUT KRYPTONITE?
LET ME THINK ABOUT IT.
KLIK
WEIRDO.
HEY, BABE! IT'S THE MAIN MAN CALLIN'. MAYBE YOU CAN HELP ME OUT WITH SOMETHING. I'M LOOKING FOR AN ESTIMATE ON A BUILDING.
TO BUILD IT?
NAW... I'M GONNA BLOW 'ER UP REAL GOOD. FER GIGGLES.
HOW 'BOUT AFTER I FRAG THIS JOINT, YOU AND I GO OUT FOR SOME BBQ?
KLIK
BADOOM
CREEP.
LONG DISTANCE? I DON'T RECOGNIZE THIS AREA CODE...
YOU HAVE ONE NEW MESSAGE.
IF YOU RECEIVE THIS MESSAGE, I'M IN URGENT NEED OF YOUR SERVICES. TO MAKE THESE LIVING CONDITIONS LESS GRIM AND HOT.
ALMIGHTY DARKSEID...NO! I WAS CALLING COLLECT... I SWEAR!
FRZZAP
KRACKLE

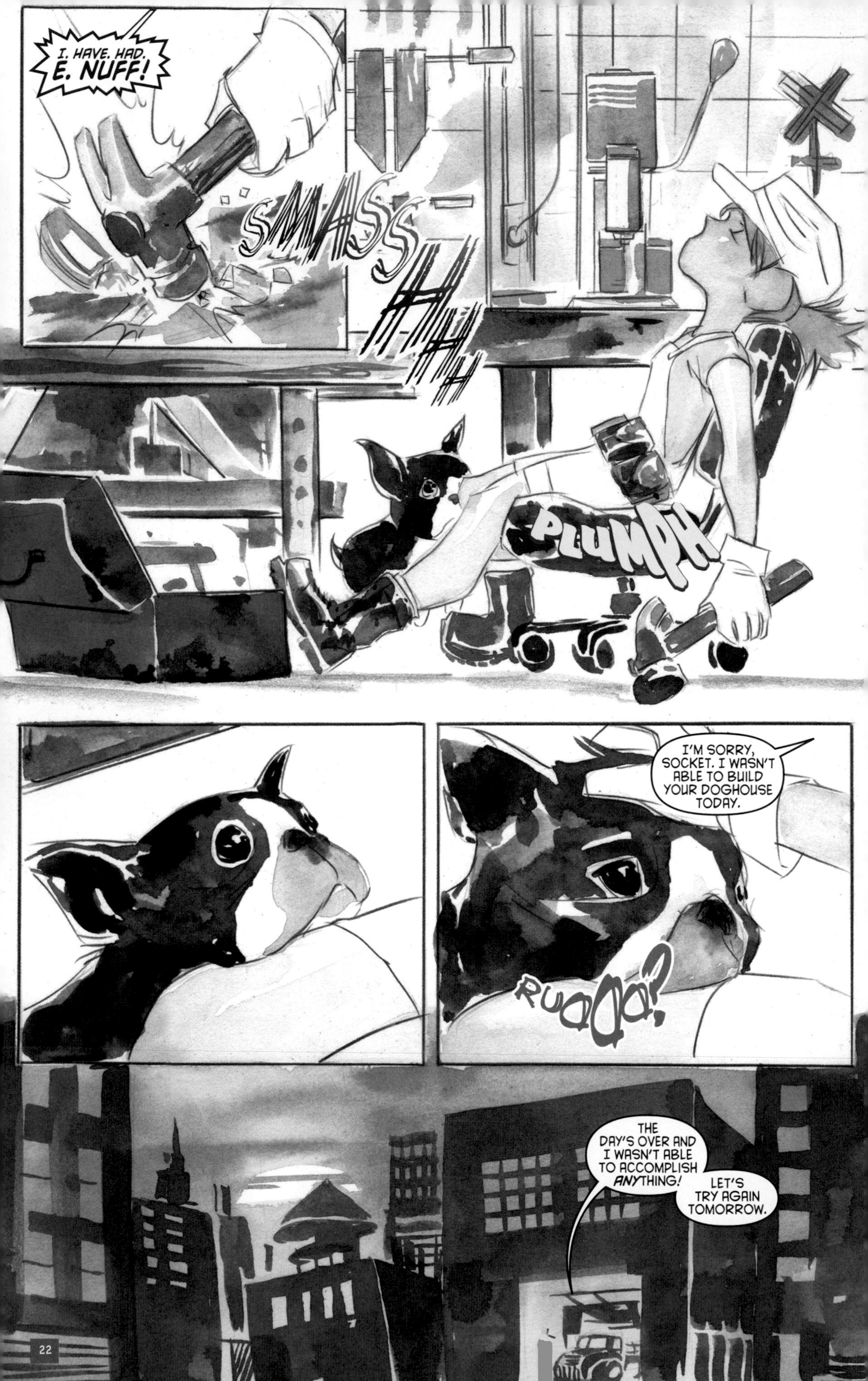
I. HAVE. HAD. E. NUFF!
SMASSHHH
PLUMPH
I'M SORRY, SOCKET. I WASN'T ABLE TO BUILD YOUR DOGHOUSE TODAY.
RUQQQ?
THE DAY'S OVER AND I WASN'T ABLE TO ACCOMPLISH ANYTHING!
LET'S TRY AGAIN TOMORROW.

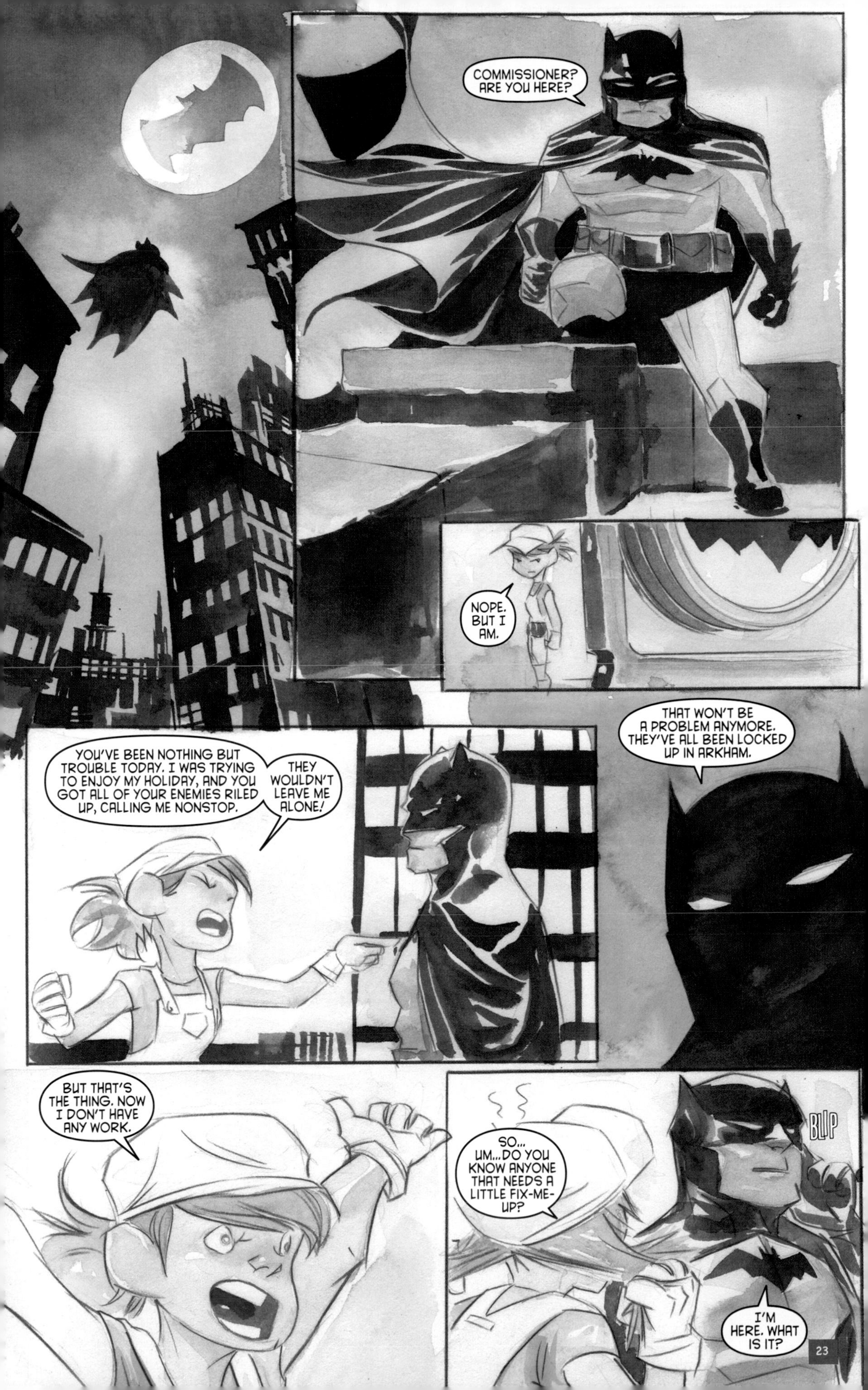
COMMISSIONER? ARE YOU HERE?
NOPE. BUT I AM.
YOU'VE BEEN NOTHING BUT TROUBLE TODAY. I WAS TRYING TO ENJOY MY HOLIDAY, AND YOU GOT ALL OF YOUR ENEMIES RILED UP, CALLING ME NONSTOP.
THEY WOULDN'T LEAVE ME ALONE!
THAT WON'T BE A PROBLEM ANYMORE. THEY'VE ALL BEEN LOCKED UP IN ARKHAM.
BUT THAT'S THE THING. NOW I DON'T HAVE ANY WORK.
SO... UM...DO YOU KNOW ANYONE THAT NEEDS A LITTLE FIX-ME-UP?
BLIP
I'M HERE. WHAT IS IT?

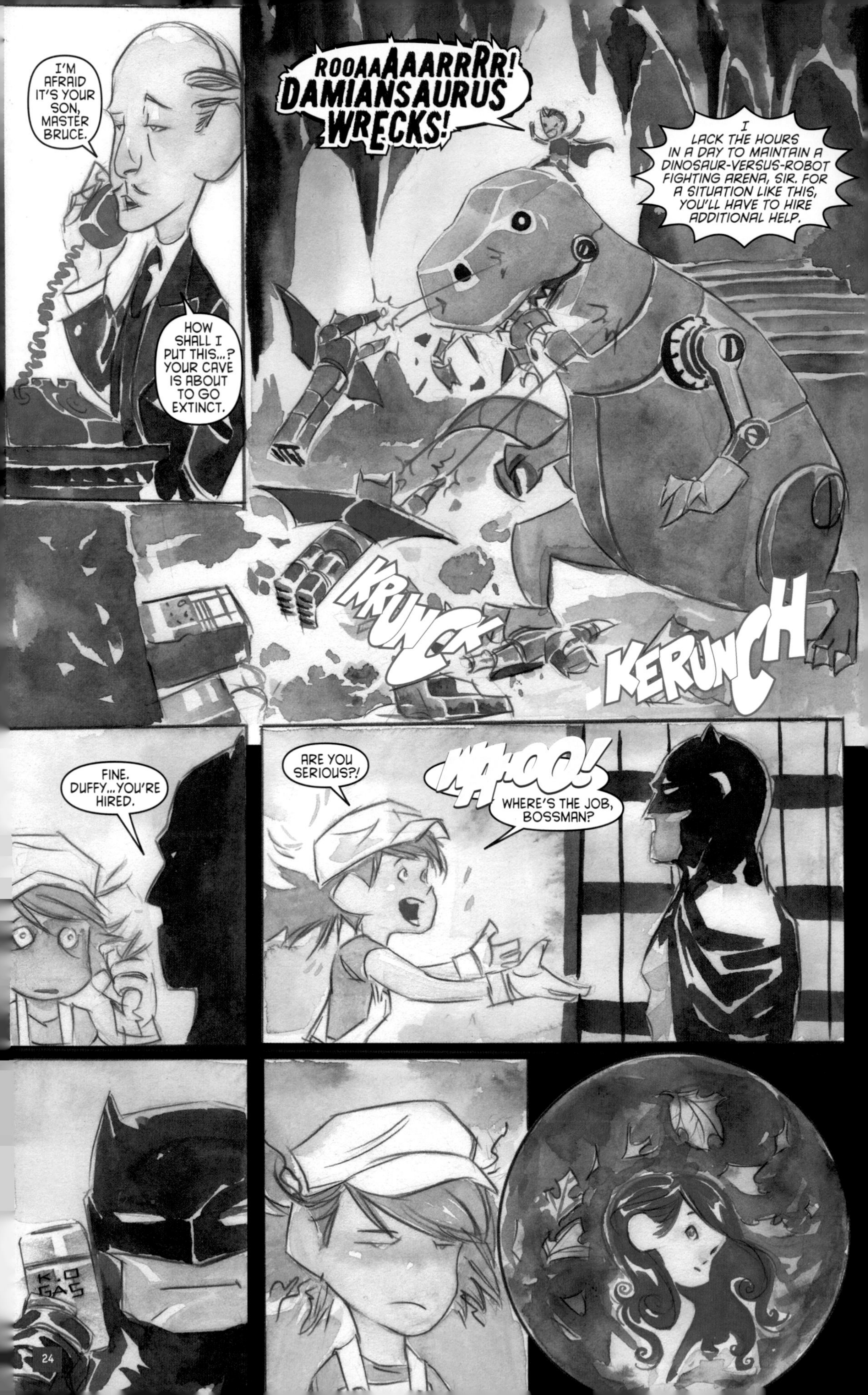
I'M AFRAID IT'S YOUR SON, MASTER BRUCE.
ROOAAAAARRRRR! DAMIANSAURUS WRECKS!
I LACK THE HOURS IN A DAY TO MAINTAIN A DINOSAUR-VERSUS-ROBOT FIGHTING ARENA, SIR. FOR A SITUATION LIKE THIS, YOU'LL HAVE TO HIRE ADDITIONAL HELP.
HOW SHALL I PUT THIS...? YOUR CAVE IS ABOUT TO GO EXTINCT.
KRUNCH
KERUNCH
FINE. DUFFY...YOU'RE HIRED.
ARE YOU SERIOUS?!
WAHOO!
WHERE'S THE JOB, BOSSMAN?
K.O GAS

CREATORS

DUSTIN NGUYEN — CO-WRITER & ILLUSTRATOR

Dustin Nguyen is an American comic artist whose body of work includes Wildcats v3.0, The Authority Revolution, Batman, Superman/ Batman, Detective Comics, Batgirl, and his creator owned project Manifest Eternity. Currently, he produces all the art for Batman: Li'l Gotham, which is also written by himself and Derek Fridolfs. Outside of comics, Dustin moonlights as a conceptual artist for toys, games, and animation. In his spare time, he enjoys sleeping, driving, and sketching things he loves.

DEREK FRIDOLFS — CO-WRITER

Derek Fridolfs is a comic book writer, inker, and artist. He resides in Gotham--present and future.

GLOSSARY

admission (ad-MISH-uhn)--the right or permission to enter a place

continuity (con-ti-NOO-uh-tee)--the quality of something that does not stop or change as time passes, or consistency of representation

eternity (ee-TER-nuh-tee)--time without end

exclusive (ek-SKLOO-siv)--available only to a few people or under particular circumstances

fascinating (FASS-uh-nay-ting)--very interesting or appealing

inspire (in-SPY-er)--if you inspire others, you make them want to do something

masquerade (mass-kuh-RAYD)--a party, dance, or other festive gathering of persons wearing masks and other disguises

principle (PRIN-suh-puhl)--an accepted or professed rule of action or conduct

puns (PUNNZ)--a humorous way of using a word or phrase so that more than one meaning is suggested

renovating (REN-uh-vay-ting)--making changes and repairs to something meant to improve its value or appearance

revamped (ree-VAMPT)--made something better or new again

VISUAL QUESTIONS & PROMPTS

1. Why is the word "dirty" italicized and in a different color than the rest of the text in Clayface's speech bubble?

SPLUTT
1
HEY, KID, BETTER WIPE YOUR FACE. 'CUZ IT LOOKS *DIRTY!*

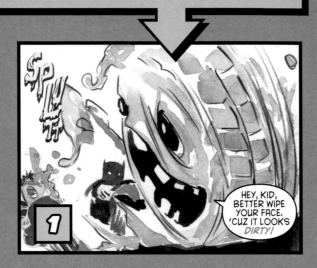

2. Why did Robin dress up as a poor imitation of Clayface? What was he trying to achieve? Reread pages 12-13 for clues.

2

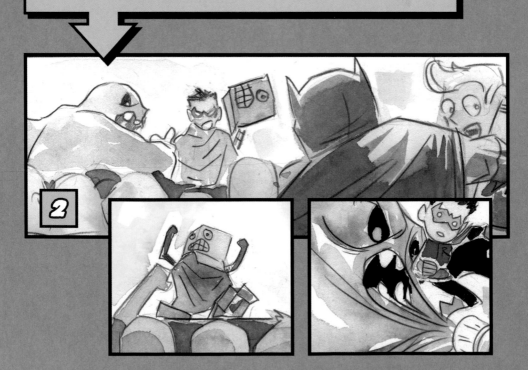

3. Why is half the room different than the other half? Hint: it has to do with someone who lives there.

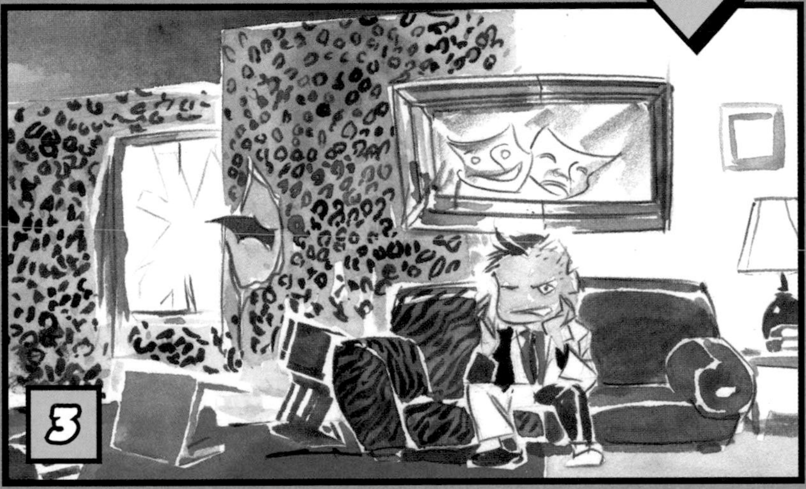

4. Why do you think Batman is going to hit Duffy with knockout gas? Reread page 24 if you aren't sure.

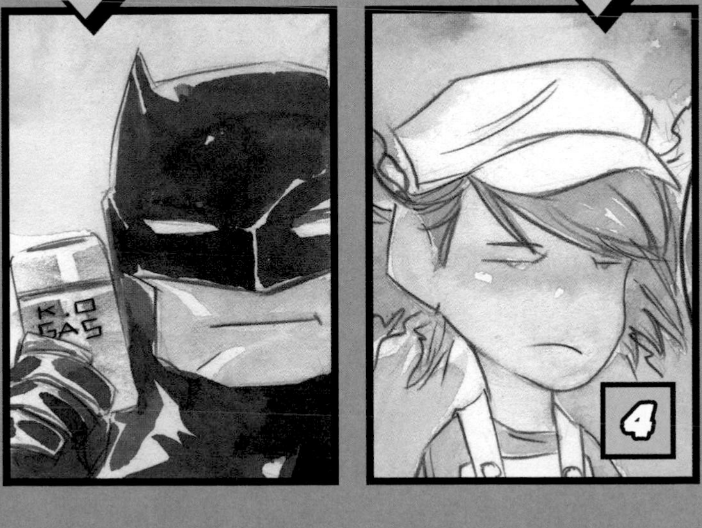
K.O
GAS

BATMAN™ LI'L GOTHAM

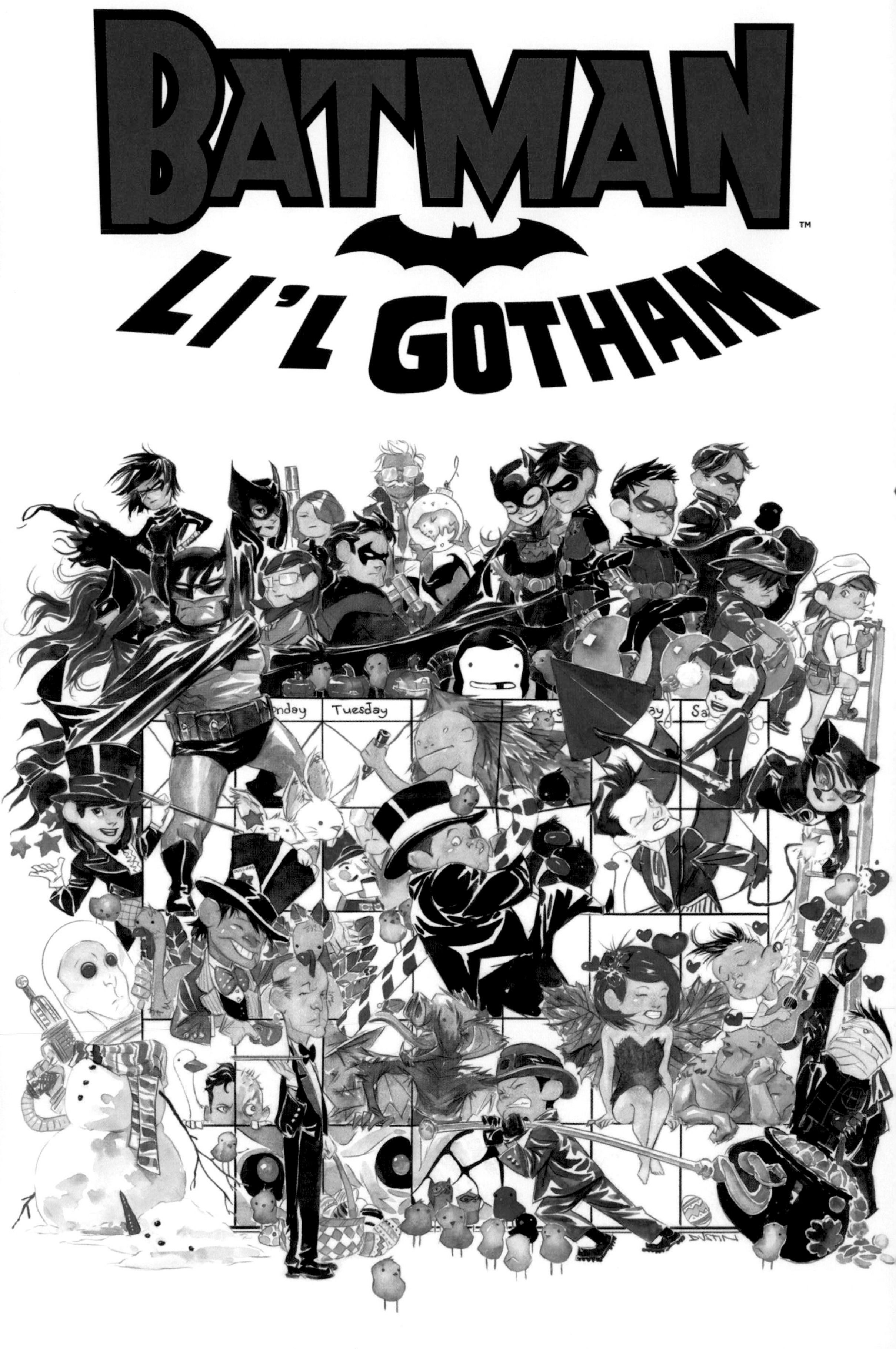
Tuesday

READ THEM ALL!

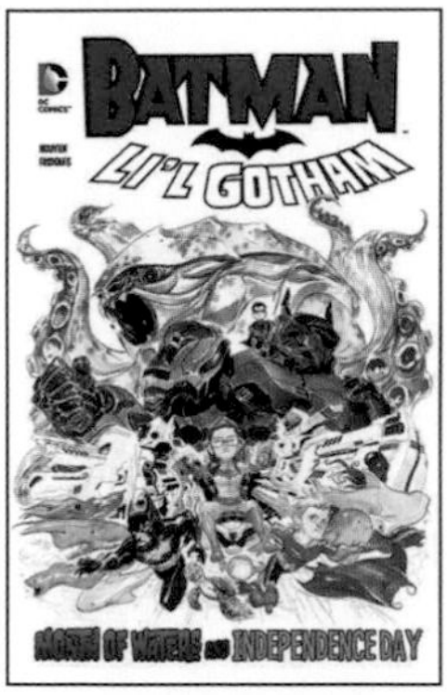
BATMAN
LI'L GOTHAM
INDEPENDENCE DAY

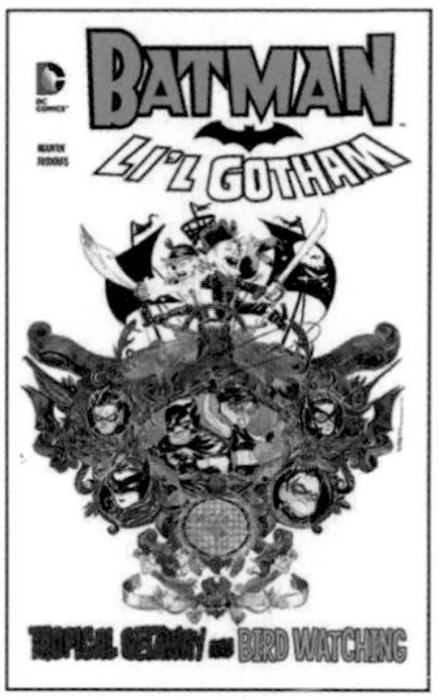
BATMAN
LI'L GOTHAM
TROPICAL GETAWAY AND BIRD WATCHING

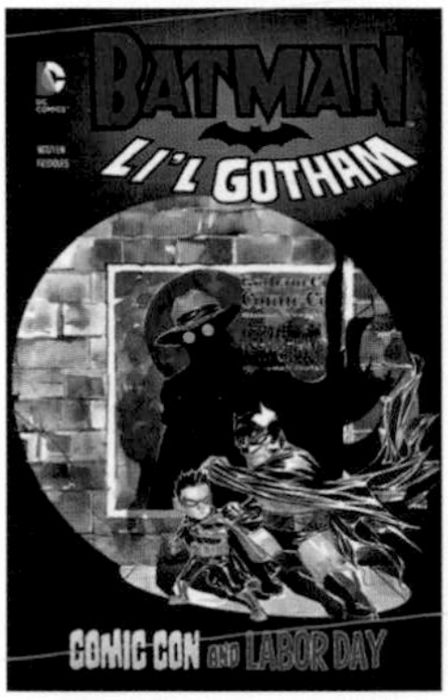
BATMAN
LI'L GOTHAM
COMIC CON AND LABOR DAY

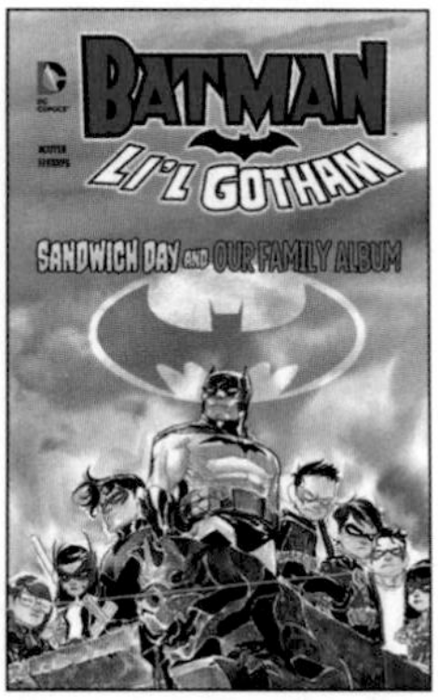
BATMAN
LI'L GOTHAM
SANDWICH DAY AND OUR FAMILY ALBUM

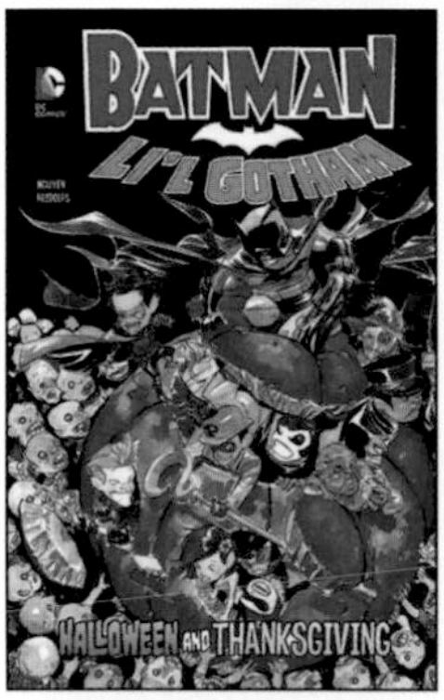
BATMAN
LI'L GOTHAM
HALLOWEEN AND THANKSGIVING

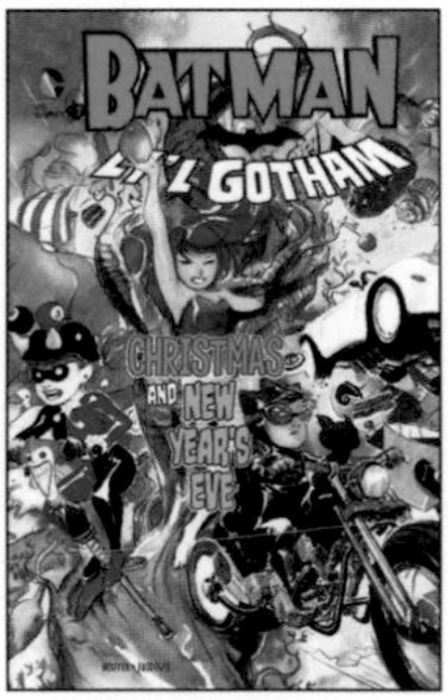
BATMAN
LI'L GOTHAM
CHRISTMAS AND NEW YEAR'S EVE

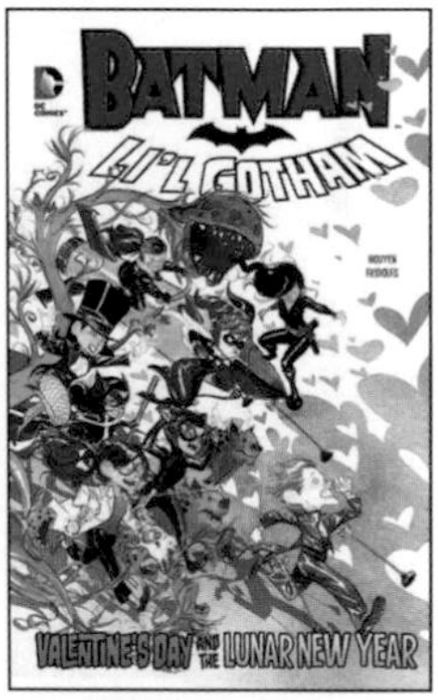
BATMAN
LI'L GOTHAM
VALENTINE'S DAY AND THE LUNAR NEW YEAR

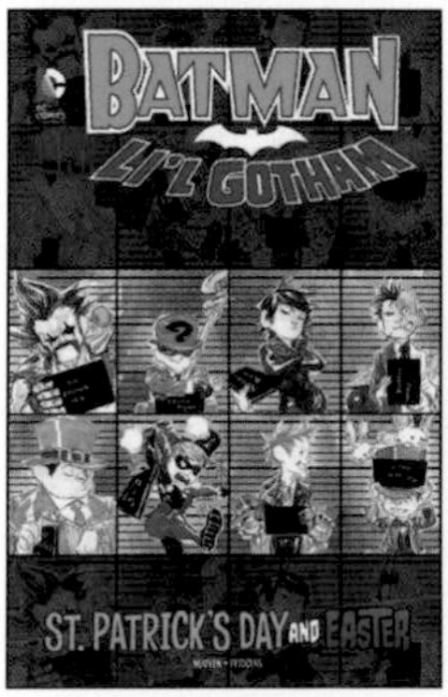
BATMAN
LI'L GOTHAM
ST. PATRICK'S DAY AND EASTER

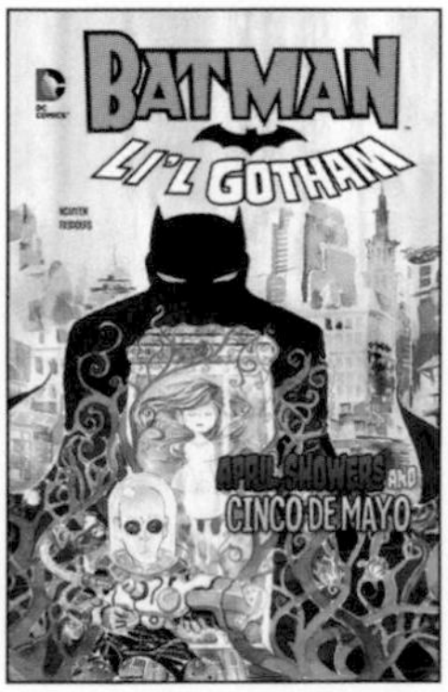
BATMAN
LI'L GOTHAM
APRIL SHOWERS AND CINCO DE MAYO

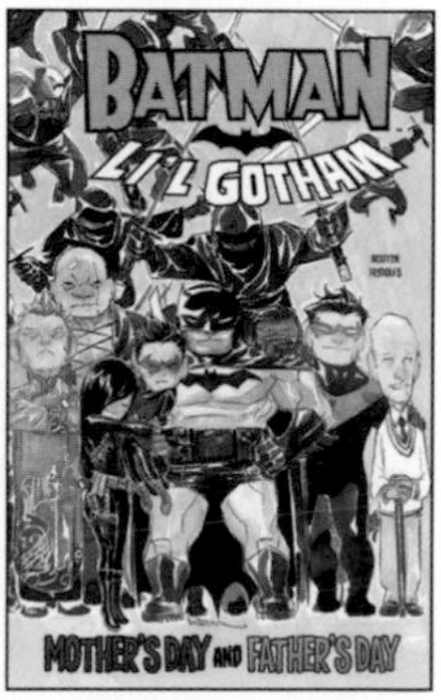
BATMAN
LI'L GOTHAM
MOTHER'S DAY AND FATHER'S DAY

BATMAN™

LI'L GOTHAM

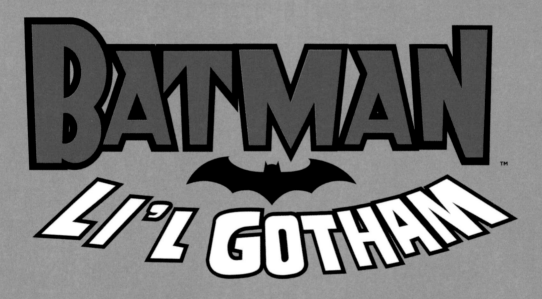